LOST IN THE LOOKING GLASS

A Retelling of Behind the Looking Glass, and What Alice Found There

Rebecca Fittery

Copyright © 2023 Rebecca Fittery

All rights reserved

The characters and events portrayed in this book are fictitious. Any similarity to real persons, living or dead, is coincidental and not intended by the author.

No part of this book may be reproduced, or stored in a retrieval system, or transmitted in any form or by any means, electronic, mechanical, photocopying, recording, or otherwise, without express written permission of the publisher.

ISBN: 978-1-7361122-9-8

Cover design created with Canva.
Map created with Inkarnate.

To my sister, Rachel, who has a heart big enough for the whole world. Being your sister is one of my favorite things about this life. Love you!

CONTENTS

Title Page
Copyright
Dedication
Map of Istoire
Prologue — 1
Chapter One — 6
Chapter Two — 12
Chapter Three — 17
Chapter Four — 24
Chapter Five — 28
Chapter Six — 36
Chapter Seven — 44
Chapter Eight — 51
Chapter Nine — 60
Chapter Ten — 69
Chapter Eleven — 77
Chapter Twelve — 85
Chapter Thirteen — 92
Chapter Fourteen — 97
Chapter Fifteen — 101

Chapter Sixteen	107
Chapter Seventeen	111
Chapter Eighteen	118
Chapter Nineteen	125
Chapter Twenty	134
Chapter Twenty-One	138
Chapter Twenty-Two	146
Chapter Twenty-Three	151
Chapter Twenty-Four	156
Chapter Twenty-Five	168
Chapter Twenty-Six	174
Chapter Twenty-Seven	179
Chapter Twenty-Eight	184
Epilogue	187
Next Book In This Series	191
Books By This Author	193
Connect With Me	201
Acknowledgements	203
About The Author	205

MAP OF ISTOIRE

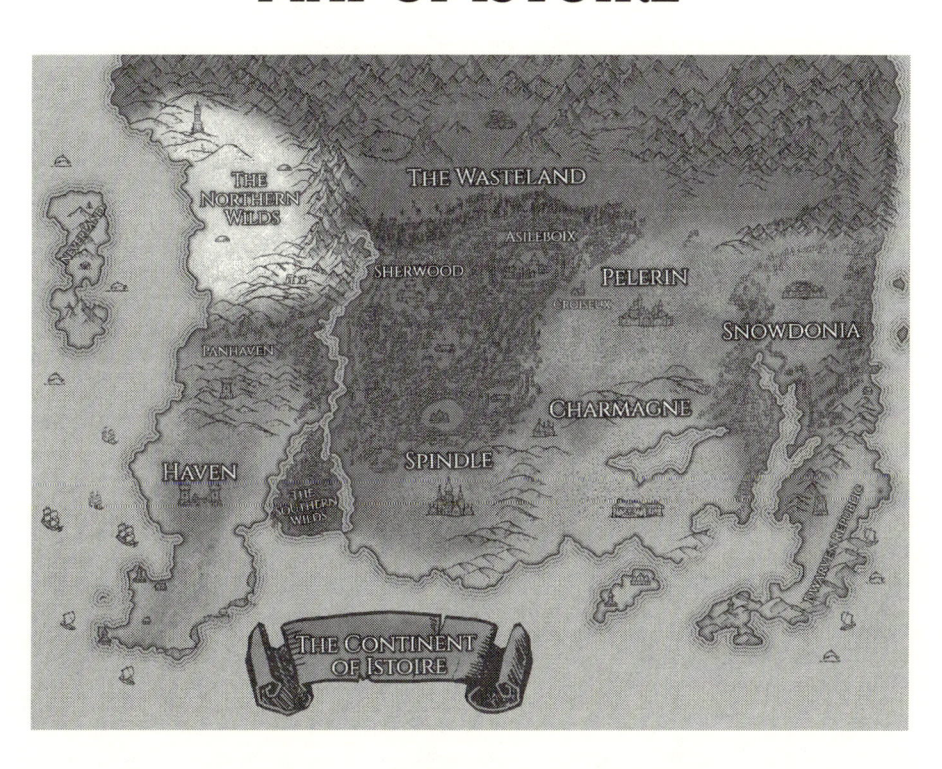

PROLOGUE

Alice looked steadily into the mirror of her painted vanity, stroking the little black kitten nestled sleepily in her arms. To the outside observer, it looked as though Alice was staring at her own face, but actually, she was wondering what it might be like to live in a world that was upside-down.

She hadn't really considered upside-down living before. She quite liked her current life and its right-side-up tendencies. All the people in it were lovely and warm, and all the things she got to do were fascinating and often fun. Even the things others complained about, like lessons (which she loved) and court events (which she loved even more), were interesting to Alice. But the most interesting thing of all had happened just a few hours ago.

Alice cared about her family a lot. At times, she even worried about them. Although she was only a teenager, and the youngest of a group of four overachieving princes and princesses, she sometimes felt like the most grown-up out of the bunch.

That's not to say Alice was too grown up to resort to spying and eavesdropping to satisfy her curiosity. She was aware that it was considered impolite and perhaps downright rude, but it did frequently come in handy. In fact, she had done both spying *and* eavesdropping in the last twenty-four hours alone, with dramatic—if not quite satisfactory—results.

She hadn't *meant* to do either, really. But she had stumbled upon a message addressed to her older sister, Persinette, and somehow or another had read it before she could look away. It was the type of thing her friends did to their sisters quite regularly, but it was the first time Alice had done it to Persinette. She had immediately withdrawn from Persi's room—having utterly forgotten why she had gone there in the first place—to ruminate on the note. Alice was one of those lucky sorts who only had to see or hear a thing once before she could commit it to memory. It made lessons easy and spying even easier.

It was a rendezvous, that much was clear, although there wasn't anything overt in the note to give it away. Persi was serious and excessively focused on her military career, certainly not the type to encourage secret meetings with a man. Besides that, she had been allowing some stuffy Lord something-or-another to court her for the past few months. The note had *not* been from him. But Alice had known that *that* courtship would come to nothing even before it started, so she was hardly surprised it wasn't from *him*.

No, what *was* surprising was that the note had been from Petro, the Prince of the Romany. Petro was good friends with all of Alice's siblings and was indeed friendly to Alice herself, but he was best friends of all with Persi. Alice drew in a thoughtful breath as she stroked the purring kitten and wondered at this turn of events.

Petro hadn't been to the palace for several years, but as he and Persi were both busy with their new careers, it was to be expected. His note confirming he would meet Persi for coffee *could* be the most natural thing in the world—two old friends catching up in the city while one was passing through. But the way he had phrased it made Alice think there was more to it, though she couldn't put her finger on why. Just her knack for seeing what others sought to conceal wriggling like a worm in her brain. She had detected a longing in it, something tremulous but true—*very* unlike the down-to-earth Petro.

Having read the note, Alice had quickly realized that she

would go to the coffee shop too. Not with Persi, obviously. As much as she and Persi got on, Persi tended to be excessively independent. She would never seek support for affairs of the heart. Persi *gave* support, but she didn't seek it.

But what could be more natural than a teenage princess quietly sneaking out to patronize a coffee shop near the university? It was the sort of thing Alice did all the time. So she collected her most unobtrusive bodyguard, a surly woman in her late fifties who passed as a companion, and dressed in her plainest set of walking clothes and arrived exactly one hour before the meeting was to take place, ready to settle in with a coffee—book in hand.

She left the coffee shop more confused than ever, several hours and *many* cups of dark roast later. Petro had come well ahead of the assigned time. He had waited for several hours afterward, finally leaving with a defeated set to his shoulders, never having noticed Alice.

But Alice had noticed him. *And* she had noticed an unmarked carriage slowing down outside the cafe before speeding off again right around the appointed time. Although the figure in the carriage had been too shadowy to see, Alice had known it was Persi.

Alice wasn't exactly a brilliant mage, but she was competent. And her brand of royal boundary magic was more human-focused than earth-focused. She knew when her family was near and how they fared. Persi had driven by, but hadn't come in.

It had been very tempting to go talk to Petro after that, but she had ultimately decided not to meddle. Petro's lovelorn face told her everything she needed to know. And although Alice loved to help, she had exactly zero experience with romantic love—not even a first kiss yet!—and feared making things worse.

When she arrived back at the palace, she had cause to doubt that decision. Her family was in an uproar. Persi had apparently broken things off with the Lord something-or-another who had courted her, accepted a commission to an intelligence unit, packed her bags, and left without waiting to say goodbye to Alice or anyone who wasn't immediately on hand.

Alice's mother had taken most of this in stride, with an air of pride for Persi's new commission mixed in with a little bewilderment at the breakup with the young lord.

"She'll be back in a few weeks at the latest," Alice told her mother. The Crown Princess shook her head.

"I wouldn't count on it, dear. They've been trying to recruit her for a specific mission for some time, and we won't see her until it's finished. I'm sorry she didn't wait to say goodbye."

Alice smiled and hugged her mother tighter than usual, artlessly ignoring the rapid-fire guesses regarding the mission that her brother, Raleigh, was launching to no one in particular. After her mother patted her on the back and turned her attention to Raleigh, Alice quickly retreated to her room to puzzle out what was going on between Persi and Petro.

She stared into the mirror, admitting to herself that she was a *little* upset her sister hadn't said goodbye. They were quite close, despite the age difference, and although Alice expected Persi wouldn't last two weeks without needing to come home and declare her undying love to Petro (as evidenced by the romantic novels Alice liked to read), she couldn't help feeling overlooked.

"And that's why it all feels a bit upside down here, kitten," she said to the purring pile of fur. "Persi's gone, and she and Petro are having a secret love affair—which always sounds dangerous to one's health if you believe the fairytales, although it usually comes out right in the end—and of course, Raleigh will be off to Deerbold Academy again in a few days."

She scratched under the kitten's chin thoughtfully, blinking at her reflection in a contemplative way. "Do you know, kitten, that my oldest brother, Edwin, fell in love with *his* best friend and married her? Persi has apparently fallen in love with *her* best friend, and it's frightened her all the way to who knows where, and I've had suspicions about Raleigh and Briar for the last year at least. They aren't showing signs of being in love quite yet, but it seems to linger in the air when I'm with them."

She blinked at her reflection. "If I'm going to complete the set,

I suppose I should find a best friend to fall in love with as well. But best friends seem so difficult to come by, at least for me. I like being on my own, you know." She held the kitten in front of her face as she had been talking, or lecturing, really. When she glanced back at the mirror, she straightened up and frowned.

The woman was back—the Lady in the Mirror. She often seemed to appear when Alice was upset. And she *was* upset, although she hadn't realized it until this moment. Things were upside down, and as much as she liked novelty, Alice *didn't* like change.

"Although I suppose you live in a sideways world, don't you, Lady?" Alice whispered, knowing the apparition wouldn't be able to talk back. It wouldn't be for lack of trying on the Lady's part, but Alice didn't know how to help her. And there had always been something about her that made Alice hold back. Her beauty was too overwhelming, her gaze too knowing, her smile too sharp. Besides that, no one else had ever seen her. Alice's attempts when she was younger to try and prove to her parents that the Lady was truly in the mirror had resulted in an emphasis on creative writing during her tutoring sessions, as well as several trips to the seaside in winter, which her grandmother thought was a cure-all for everything.

The memory of that misunderstanding gave Alice a little jolt of temper. Without stopping to think, she raised her hand and flung a surge of boundary magic at the mirror—right at the Lady's face. It was downright strange how she would appear when Alice felt low and how no one else had ever seen her. Alice wanted her out—wanted to feel like she wasn't being watched.

To her surprise, the rudimentary spell—or at least the raw power behind it—seemed to work. The Lady flickered, then vanished. The only people in the mirror now were the reflections of Alice and the kitty—how it should be.

Still, Alice wondered. What lay in that mirror world where the Lady lived?

CHAPTER ONE

Alice - Four Years Later

"Well, that was either my stupidest moment or my finest," I muttered to myself, clutching the shimmering blanket I had purloined from Cara's cottage around my shoulders. I had grabbed it before stepping through her dark mirror and into the Dreamland, proving I hadn't been entirely impulsive. Apparently the fabric was uniquely suited to help people move through the Dreamworld safely and unseen.

"I suppose I should have looked through the pile for one better suited as a cape." Instead, I was left trying to stretch the blanket far enough that it would cover me from my head all the way to my ankles. It was barely long enough. "I wish I had my actual cape," I muttered at the shimmery magic cloth. I had left my best formal cape back in Cara's cottage—a sky-blue velvet that matched my eyes perfectly. Of course, it was as poorly suited for adventure as the demure white silk ballgown I still wore. As a debutante, I was forced to wear white to every ball, no matter that it made me look like a ghost with consumption.

The blanket began to shimmer in a slightly conciliatory way, and I blinked at it, then gasped.

"Oh, you clever thing!" It had swirled from a cobwebby gray into a misty sky-blue—almost the exact shade as my cape.

"That's very kind of you," I told it fondly. "Perhaps you could teach Briar Rose's cape to—" I broke off, remembering why I came.

Looking up, I scanned the area wildly, then grinned as I caught sight of my friend. *Sister-in-law*, I reminded myself. *And the main reason why I'm here. Raleigh would die if anything happened to her. And I would too. And Briar said she's going to find where Persi is—I want to find her too.*

The three of us, Raleigh, Briar, and myself—along with two of our bodyguards of course—had traveled through the night to the infamous Sleep Fairy's cottage. Cara, the Sleep Fairy, had been skeptical at first, but after Briar had explained the vision that brought us there, she had agreed to help Briar enter the Dreamworld to find answers. Raleigh had charged me with guarding Briar. I knew he had meant for me to stay in the room in the cottage, but a sudden urge made me step through the dark mirror—a desire to help my new sister-in-law finally find my sister. The only problem was, Briar and Cara had left their bodies back in the physical world, and sent their spirits into the Dreamworld. I had stepped through, body and all. *I may not have thought all that through*, I admitted to myself privately.

I opened my mouth to explain my presence as Briar shot me a puzzled look. Before I could say anything, a rustling and crunching sounded off to my left, as if something huge were running through the underbrush. I snapped my eyes toward the noise and felt a physical wave of terror sweep over me, rushing through my chest, weakening my knees, and tingling its way out of my toes.

Horror. There was no other way to describe the creature I saw clawing its way through the nondescript scrubby wasteland in the distance. Scaly gray skin stretched over a sharp framework of bones that made my own skin feel tight and itchy. Razor-sharp teeth crowded its enormous maw, promising violence and a painful death. Its eyes glowed like embers as they passed over me, searching for something or someone. I tightened my grip on the dream-woven cloth I wore. *Thank the Shepherds, it can't see me.*

As the thought crossed my mind, its face snapped toward me, as if looking straight at me. My whole body trembled—no, my entire being—under the scrutiny of its attention. The creature emanated wrath and rage and violence so potently it was suffocating.

Please don't come for me, I thought tremulously. But, of course, it did—moving toward me with a lumbering step. I wanted to run, but my legs were jelly, and my feet seemed rooted to the ground. *How I wish I hadn't come.*

Of course, that thought sparked a small memory in a back corner of my mind as to why I *had* come, which reminded me that Briar was nearby, and if the horrible creature came over to eat me, it would see Briar as well and eat her as dessert, and then this whole adventure would be horribly short—not to mention devastating to our families.

More to save her skin than my own, my feet begrudgingly took a step. I willed the monster to focus on me as I moved, and it seemed to work, its menacing gaze following my movements as it picked up speed to follow.

The closer it got, the more enormous it seemed. *How I wish I were smaller—as small as a worm! Then I wouldn't be noticed.* Transfiguring didn't seem to be an option at the moment—given the fact that I never had lessons on it from my old governess, and I was too scared to try and reverse engineer a spell as I ran—so my feet kept lurching forward, away from Briar, who was, thankfully, out of sight by now, and toward whatever lay in the lumpy, dim darkness ahead.

Although it probably was only a few handfuls of seconds, my lurching escape felt like an eternity. My ballgown and makeshift cloak tangled around me as if to aid the monster's triumph. Every noise it made behind me sent a vision of the horrible creature chomping its teeth around my neck. I shrieked as a blast of warm air hit my back, wishing desperately that I was safe at home instead of lost in the Dreamworld.

As soon as I thought about it, a familiar-looking grand castle appeared before me. A sudden hope that it would provide me a safe place to hide from the ravening monster still crashing through whatever undergrowth existed in the Dreamland behind me gave me a burst of speed. My almost athletic sprint brought me through the grand double doors of the castle, which were standing open oddly enough, though no guards manned their posts, and into a dimly lit grand entrance. When I turned to slam the front doors of the mansion shut, I pulled up short, finding they were already closed, though I hadn't heard them slam shut, nor was there anyone nearby who could have done it.

I blinked, then took a step backward. "Well, I suppose it's a barrier between me and that...that...thing, so I'll be grateful for it." Drawing in a deep breath, I turned back around to find a way deeper into the castle and put additional walls between me and danger. But as I took a few more steps into the entryway, I drew in a breath, my eyebrows drawing together in puzzlement.

It was *my* entryway. Or rather, the entrance hall of my ancestral castle in Dryfaeston, where I lived with my parents and grandparents. It was precisely the same as when I had last left—even down to the Yuletide decorations draped around the corners. *This* version of the castle seemed a bit dusty—*or not dusty,* I realized, *just sleepy, which **feels** like it should be dusty.* I shook my head at the thought. In any event, it was dark and dull, unlike the castle in *real* life, which was always light and sparkling with magic-fueled candles and lamps and an army of servants who kept it clean and ready for whichever state envoy or powerful courtier was slated to appear that day.

I shook myself and began walking—having not *completely* forgotten the horrible monster that had chased me into the castle in the first place, though I had heard neither a peep nor a roar of dismay from beyond the closed front doors. *Perhaps it had forgotten my existence,* I thought optimistically, then hesitated a moment in front of the main staircase, weighing which direction I should go. After brief consideration, I decided *not* to go peek at what my room might look like in the Dreamworld. "It would be *too* strange. No doubt I'd have nightmares about it when I get back to the real world."

Instead, my feet led me on a wandering ramble through the ground floor rooms, which were *exactly* the same as the ones at home, except as lifeless and dull as the entrance hall. The skirts of my ballgown kept threatening to trip me, competing stoutly for the most annoying garment with my makeshift cape, which kept slipping off my shoulders despite my hand clutching it tightly in place.

I slowed to a stop as I meandered through one of the drawing rooms near the public entertaining spaces, having completely regained my breath and all but forgotten the strange monster that had chased me into the palace. This room was one we kept solely for our family's use, at least in the real world. We all needed a cozy escape during public events, and as children, it had been a refuge to play games and study while still being near our parents during an event. Its soft couches and cluttered collection of beloved objects made it as homey a place as could be in a palace. Here in this Dreamworld, it was lackluster and dull like all the other rooms. I stopped beside a chess set—an exact replica of the one I played with my father and mother regularly—a beautiful cut glass set with alternating glass and mirrored squares, although the mirrored parts on this version seemed to swirl with dark shapes.

My hand drifted out to pick up one of the pawns, but stopped short, hovering with a reluctance that seemed to settle deeper into my bones with every passing moment. Something about this palace that mirrored my home filled me with dread.

It's the stillness. Our house is alive with activity, so much so that it seems like a living entity itself. This version seems like a corpse in comparison. Maybe it wouldn't feel so ominous if someone were with me to explore.

As soon as the thought crossed my mind, a melodic swell of music reached my ears, accompanied by a muted tittering of voices—sounds I recognized as proof of occupation from the grand ballroom down the hall. I blinked a few times, certain that the ballroom hadn't been occupied when I first turned into this wing of the castle.

"But it seems to be now," I said aloud to the empty room. "Maybe a mirror version of my family is hosting a ball."

I wasn't sure I wanted to meet a mirror version of my family, but my feet seemed disinclined to agree, moving toward the music with rhythmic steps.

"Besides," I muttered, "it *would* be interesting to meet the mirror version of yourself if only to see yourself clearly." I looked down at my dragging ballgown, the hem still a stark white, even though I had dragged it through who knew what running from the monster. "And I *am* still dressed for a ball, after all."

Still, my heart fluttered like a kaleidoscope of butterflies with every step I took toward the haunting music.

CHAPTER TWO

Peter

"This is a waste of time," Wendy complained as she gazed across the ballroom, leaning next to me on a silk-covered wall at the back. "Let's get back to the mission."

I didn't respond, my eyes tracing the masked dancers without seeing them. She was right in that the nightly ball held even less interest than usual, but I wasn't here to work. Just being away from Neverland—and my mother, the Grand Pixie—meant I was content. Here at the ghostly masquerade, I was disguised even further—a simple knight arrayed in elegant white armor.

Wendy pushed off the wall, turning toward me and looping her hands around one of my biceps. "Come on, this is boring anyway," she insisted, managing to pout and smile at the same time.

I kept my arms folded across my chest, reluctant to give in to her, but shot her a half-smile anyway. "You go on if you want. I'm staying here for now."

She shifted her hands downward, tugging at my wrist until she could claim my hand, her face slipping into a real pout. "You choose staying at this party over continuing our mission *again*?" she whined. "You're the next Grand Pixie of Neverland. You have to start taking mending the island seriously. You'll become a shriveled self-centered beast if you don't."

My smile threatened to slip off my face, but I forced it wider instead. *If I stay calm, she'll get bored and wander off.* "You've known me a long time, Wendy. Taking care of *me* has always been my first priority. And tonight, I want to party, not search for a needle in a haystack." I continued, letting a hint of mockery enter my voice, "But don't feel like you have to stay and babysit me. You go off on your noble quest—just make sure you reapply the pixie dust every so often. I'll come find you when it's time to go."

She searched my face for a moment, still clinging to my hand. Her pout slipped into a more honest expression, one that had been growing in her eyes lately. It held longing and heartsickness—and despair. My lips twisted into a sneer involuntarily, and although I forced them back into my usual wide smile, I knew she caught it. Without another word, she turned and flounced away, her ponytail swinging with her head held high, even as anger tightened the lines of her shoulders.

I sighed in relief as she left the room. "I'll have to deal with that soon if I don't want it to blow up in my face," I muttered to myself, folding my arms back over my chest and letting my eyes wander over the crowd again. Wendy and I had been friends since we were children, and although I had enjoyed her attention and the flirtation we had in our teenage years, I had never promised anything more. She knew my mother's plans for my marriage—even as she knew the lengths I was considering to escape those plans. But I had never led her to believe we could be together. If she let herself think rationally for a minute, she'd know we'd never work. Staying friends with her became more irritating every day.

I shook my head. *I'll figure that out when I'm back on Neverland.* Right now, I just wanted to enjoy the dance. It had happened every night for almost a month and proceeded the same way each time. As the dancers filed in from some portal, they were announced by a fancy majordomo. The first dance started after all had entered, led by the king and the current lady of honor

—which seemed to change every night—before the rest of the company joined them. After the first dance, the king retreated to his dais, accompanied by his lady of honor. Sometimes she remained with him the entire night; sometimes she was sent away after a time. The rest of the guests danced unceasingly for hours until dawn approached, and the king made some announcement. Instead of relief that the dance was over, the dancers seemed dejected at his announcement, streaming out of the ballroom and back to whatever land they came from with an air of despair. It all formed an oddly fascinating puzzle, and I was determined to understand what was going on.

I had been attending for weeks—whenever I could get away to the Dreamworld without being caught by my mother or a busybody member of the Court of Faeries. It was the sort of distraction from my boring studies and princely duties that I needed—low cost to myself and interesting without being all-consuming. The dancers could see but not hear me, nor I them. I assumed they spoke a different language since I couldn't even guess their words when their mouths moved, but I got on by pretending I couldn't speak when needed. So far, it had worked, and I hadn't attracted any real suspicions that I didn't actually belong.

I bowed as a lady and her chaperone passed by but made no move to ask for a dance as I normally would. Wendy's accusation had put me in a sullen mood, and I didn't want to deal with a nervous partner who I couldn't communicate with. Instead, I relaxed against the wall again and shot a glance at the king. While the other dancers were decked in the usual finery, their king was outfitted in a luxury that was simple, but obscene. Gold dripped over every surface of his clothing and crept up the high collar of his tunic. Each finger bore at least one ring, and the earrings lining the shell of his ears were gold as well. Dark circles—either born of insomnia or created by artifice, I couldn't tell—surrounded his eyes and made their dark depths seem bottomless. The entire effect was beautiful but sinister, and although he sat looking bored to tears every night, even the most subtle movement on his part sent a ripple among the dancers as if they were a school of fish preparing to scatter before a shark.

That they were real people, my magic had confirmed easily enough. Some king somewhere on the mainland had obviously gathered enough magic to create a small world of his own within the Dreamworld. And although my pixie magic allowed me to access the Dreamworld too, it also kept me slightly separate from the experience created by magic from the mainland—an effect, no doubt, of the sundering between worlds that my ancestors had created so long ago. Not even in the realm of Dreams could I get to the mainland.

Still, the veil between us is thin in this place, whatever Wendy thinks. The fact that I can see and interact with them proves it. Perhaps this is the way I can break the magic and bring Neverland back into the world. I laughed. *Wouldn't it be wonderful if my self-centered partying led to the healing of Neverland? Wendy would have a stroke.* And if I could manage healing Neverland, there would be no need for me to marry Lily—the Shepherd's daughter with magic to rival those ancient beings who helped create our world—and no need to save our failing pixie magic.

"If I could just figure out what you're up to," I muttered at the king, staring at him with dislike, "maybe I could figure out how you're doing this. And if I knew your spell, I could find a way to break into it."

As I stared at the king, a sudden flare of magic thrilled through the Dreamworld and overwhelmed my senses for a second. It felt like a gust of spring air rattling barren branches on a frostbitten morning, and it left an electric taste in my mouth. The sensation lasted only the briefest moment, but the after-effects eddied through me, sparkling with energy and disintegrating the sluggishness that had accompanied me all day.

I turned toward the magic's source, desperately wanting to see what it was. It seemed I was the only person in the ballroom affected by it. The dancers hadn't missed a beat in their swirling display, and no one else turned as I had. Whatever it was seemed to be closer to my plane of existence in the Dreamworld than theirs.

A surge of greed set my feet into motion. Whatever magic that was—*or was it a person?* I felt sure it had been life magic that I had felt, a bright, burning life that had wholly entered the Dreamworld without proper protection spells. *Whoever it was obviously had power, if less sense than a rabbit. His hubris in refusing to cloak it would be the most entertaining event in Dreamworld for a long time.* The dance would wait for another day.

CHAPTER THREE

Alice

"Did I imagine a ball into existence?" I muttered to myself as I walked across the sitting room. "Maybe that's how this place works. You imagine a thing, and it appears, as long as you imagine hard enough." I pursed my lips. In that case, I wish I had a set of instructions or something to show me how it all works. Nothing happened. "It's the least a magical world could do," I admonished, glaring at the walls of the familiar but not-quite-right room.

A skittering noise sounded behind me, and I whirled around in alarm. After scanning the room several times, I suddenly realized the noise was coming from the chessboard I had recently examined. Frowning, I took several steps back toward it, then stopped in amazement.

"The pieces are moving," I breathed, bending closer to peer down at their awkward movements. When I had been examining the board previously, I hadn't noticed anything extraordinary about them, but now they had all transformed.

"There are the White King and Queen," I whispered, then blinked as I caught sight of the two white rooks strolled by them, arm in arm, and I could have sworn—yes, they were actually whispering to each other. Most of the pawns were fighting with each other, and I could just make out their tiny voices issuing tiny taunts regarding which squares they were inhabiting at the moment. The Red King dashed by, trailing an odd assortment of his court—and several from the White Court as well, which would have made more sense on a checkers board instead of a chess board. In direct opposition to her partner, the Red Queen was quite stationary, still standing in her starting square and ignoring the chaos of the rest of the board.

"You're not a very organized set of courts, you know," I muttered to the entrancing scene of scurrying game pieces. "If this were the *real* world, my grandmother would set you to rights in a moment. Although, since there are already two queens on the board, I'm not sure how she would enter the game. There can't be *three* queens, can there?" I nibbled on the inside of my cheek, considering. "In real life, there certainly couldn't be more than two. But, as this is the Dreamworld, I suppose Grandmother could create a third queen for a game of chess."

I glanced again at the pieces, then leaned closer to try and catch what the White Queen was saying—her look of despair piercing my heart.

"My poor daughter, my Lily!" she whimpered, winding her way through the pawns and players, the White King now trailing her silently. "Where is she? Is she safe? Has she been discovered yet?" Her pitiful lament cut to my heart, and I looked around the game board for a—*now, what would the daughter of a chess piece look like? There aren't any princesses in chess.* As I traced the progress of the White Queen, who never seemed to find her daughter, I tried to picture what a chess princess would look like —*a sort of cross between the king and queen pieces, except her crown shouldn't outshine the queen. But where would she stand on the board?*

As I allowed my mind to wander, the chessboard began shaking, and I felt—just faintly—a subtle stirring of magic that I realized had occurred the other two times I had seemed to change the Dreamworld with simply a wish. This time it was laced with something potent—almost a *scent* of magic instead of a feel. It smelled cloying, like roses and copper.

I reached out to steady the gameboard but reeled back as a hand struck my cheek, utterly startling me and driving away the stir of magic and the scent of roses.

I blinked, reaching up to touch my cheek where the sting of the slap was already fading, although my alarm hadn't. I turned, swiftly, then blinked in amazement to find a young demi-god in white armor standing directly before me, furious sage-green eyes drilling down into mine and a frown marring his handsome face. He reached forward and gripped my shoulders with strong hands, giving me a little shake.

"Are you crazy?" he demanded, his voice laced with a magic that tingled across my skin—not a spell, just wild power as I had never encountered outside the most sacred of magic spaces. The feel of it was intoxicating, though not quite comfortable. The hands gripping my shoulders tightened again, and I realized the man in front of me was waiting for an answer.

Having grown up in a court full of wealthy nobles who spent fortunes on their beauty and had hitherto thought myself immune to outward appearance. I should be angry with this person, or at least irritated given that he had first slapped me and was now squeezing my shoulders, but as I blinked up at him I discovered I was neither. It was utterly stupefying to be in the presence of—let alone be the focus of—such an arresting display of youthful, masculine beauty.

Still, it's not as though he can help how pretty he is. I frowned, wondering briefly if he was using a glamour, but a quick inspection made me think he wasn't. I could usually spot such magic straight away. I drew in a steadying breath. Still feeling knocked a bit sideways by the entire situation, I decided to mind my manners until I could figure out who exactly this person was.

"Pardon me, did you ask me something?" I inquired politely, blinking the stupor out of my eyes.

"Did I—" the man spluttered and then broke off, the frown on his forehead becoming thunderous. "I had asked if you were *crazy*," he continued finally, his hands still digging into the thin sleeves of my ballgown, "but I think I already have my answer.

Your brains must be addled beyond belief."

I raised my eyebrows at his rudeness but determined that I simply wouldn't play into his theatrics. *It will only feed the drama, and I'd rather get rid of him so I can continue with my exploration.*

"Well, I certainly heard worse accusations from my governess when I was a child," I replied as agreeably as I could, "and I daresay I haven't grown out of any of my bad habits—so I won't disagree with you. I *will*, however, point out that *I* am not the one squeezing a person's shoulders to death—nor did I strike your face." I pasted a mild expression of censure on my face. He let go of my shoulders as if stung.

"I only slapped you because you were so entranced by that silly game," he said defensively. "I—I *did* call out to you first, of course. And I tried to tug your sleeve. But when you reached for the gameboard, I had to resort to *something* to snap you out of it." He had a sulky expression on his face that somehow managed to be annoying and beautiful at the same time.

"Well, I'm sorry I didn't hear you, but I think that's a bit of a drastic thing to do when I was only going to steady the playing board, don't you?"

The demi-god's pout turned into a look of scorn as he scoffed and folded his arms across his chest, the motion drawing my eyes and making me scoff internally. *Disgustingly muscular, of course, though rangy in build. Those aren't the hands of a warrior. Do demi-gods even need to exercise to stay in shape? Maybe they spring from the ocean fully formed in manly perfection and spend their days sneering at us mortals.*

"It was laced with Shepherd's magic, obviously," his strident —but somehow still attractive—tone interrupted my thoughts. "Couldn't you sense that? You'd be a fool to trifle with such a spell."

I shook my head, my thoughts a bit sluggish. *Maybe I am turning into an idiot. There's something in the air here.* I paused as something occurred to me. *Is there even air here?* Too disturbed to probe that thought further, I refocused on the conversation.

"No, of course, I couldn't sense that it was a Shepherd's spell—they've been gone for thousands of years!" I looked at him with suspicion. "How could *you* sense it anyway?"

A flash of chagrin crossed his face, but it was quickly wiped away as what seemed to be his usual arrogance returned. "I can detect any flavor of magic. For example, I can tell *you* have magic, though of the human variety, not *faery*."

I gasped. "Fairy magic! That explains it!" I swept my eyes over him in newfound fascination. "The power that's oozing out of you is dizzying." I laughed out loud, pressing my hands to my cheeks in amusement. "I actually thought you were a demi-god at first. How ridiculous is that?"

A pleased expression crossed his face, only to be replaced with disgruntlement at my obvious mirth. "How do you know I'm *not* a demi-god? Some of the Shepherds did have children with mortals, you know."

I folded my hands in front of me. "*Are* you a demi-god, then?"

"No," he admitted self-consciously.

I watched him for a moment, wondering what to make of him. He was a bundle of contradictions—powerful magic wrapped up in a boyish tendency toward defensiveness. He seemed mature and young at the same time, though I guessed he was somewhere around my age—just recently into adulthood.

I stirred at a sudden thought. "If you have fairy magic, do you have wings?" I asked excitedly. "Can I see them? All the old fairytales say that fairies have wings!"

He cast a stormy look in my direction. "No, I don't. And don't you know it's rude to ask that?" he demanded. "And besides, it *faeries*, not *fairies*. You keep saying it wrong."

I unfolded my hands and put them on my hips. "How can it possibly be rude to ask about wings if you don't have any? And what exactly is the difference in how I'm saying *fairy* to how you're saying *faerie*?"

The knight scoffed. "Well, if you can't hear the nuance in it straight away, I don't suppose I can explain it to you. You just have to try better."

I frowned at him, then softened my stance. Although I suspected there was no real difference in our pronunciations, if there was one that I simply couldn't hear, I suppose it would be annoying for him. *He must not be a true fairy—I mean, faerie—just a construct made by a faerie. I bet he feels self-conscious about it.* "I didn't mean any offense about the wings thing, you know," I said contritely. "I didn't realize it was rude. I'm sorry."

He straightened his shoulders and cast another arrogant glance my way. "I wouldn't expect *you* to know of the ways of faeries, young lady," he replied condescendingly.

I gave a short sigh that would have my governess despairing at my manners, but I couldn't help it. I was losing interest in the conversation and didn't want to spend my time here arguing with a stranger. *There's a whole world to explore! And, of course, I'll have to find Briar Rose soon, too.*

"I suppose you're right," I conceded. "Now, please excuse me. I really must be going." I thought about curtsying but dismissed it in favor of a regal nod—something I felt I could pull off since I was still in my ballgown—and turned to go out the door I came in. Even though that door led away from the music of the ballroom, which still called to my curious nature, I didn't want this faerie following me in and making a nuisance of himself. There should be another entrance around the corner where I could slip in on my own.

"Oh no, you don't," he said brazenly, grabbing my arm and tugging me back around.

Although I stumbled as he pulled me back, I quickly regained my feet despite the low heels I was wearing. "Have you no manners at *all*?" I demanded with real exasperation. I tugged my arm out of his grasp in an unladylike manner and glared at him.

"Not really, no," he admitted with a wide grin, but changed to a frown and stepped closer. "But seriously, you can't go running off. You aren't protected at all. I could feel your life-magic oozing everywhere, even from the ballroom—and that's technically a different plane of existence than this one. If you don't cloak yourself soon, you'll call all the worst denizens of the

Dreamworld to you, like moths to a flame."

I shivered, realizing I had let my silver-spun blanket drop to the floor by the chessboard at some point. I hurriedly bent to pick it up and pull it around my shoulders. The man watched my movements, reaching out to touch the fabric where I held it closed at my neck.

"That will help, but it would be better if you had the proper magic to guard you," he said. "I don't want you to get hurt," he added as an afterthought. He blinked rapidly for a moment, seeming almost surprised at his own words.

"Is that why that thing was chasing me earlier?" I asked in a low voice. He gave me a questioning look. "It was horrible looking," I continued, searching for the words to convey what it looked like. "All gray and leathery with these wings—" I broke off in exasperation. "Oh, I do wish I had an encyclopedia—or better yet, a bestiary—of all the creatures in here so I could *show* you the one I saw."

No sooner had I said the words than a huge, heavy tome appeared in my hands. I promptly dropped it on the floor with a thunderous clap. It fell open to a page near the middle of the book. A picture dominated the page—a picture of the very monster that had chased me.

"That's it!" I exclaimed, pointing to the open book and carefully pronouncing the script next to it. "The Jabberwocky!"

CHAPTER FOUR

Peter

This girl is going to die, and she's going to take me with her. I was glad I still had my masquerade costume on, disguising me as a simple white knight instead of a faerie prince. If I attracted the attention of the wrong sorts in the Dreamworld, my disguise might help protect me when I had to make a quick getaway. And the Jabberwocky was the worst sort of attention there was.

"You're saying *that* was the monster chasing you earlier?" I asked, pointing to the picture in the book to confirm that I hadn't misunderstood her—and giving her a chance to double-check that she hadn't mistaken the picture. She looked like the type of air-headed noble maiden that danced attendance on me at court—while I danced circles around their simple little minds. *I bet she didn't even see the creature, just a misshapen branch. She'd be dead if she happened to stumble past it while leaking her life-magic everywhere.*

Baby-blue eyes grave, she nodded solemnly. The lack of hysteria in their depths confirmed my suspicion that her mind was as empty as the azure skies her eyes mimicked.

"Okay," I said slowly, not wanting to alarm her, but finding myself oddly reluctant to abandon her to the surely short and brutal fate that awaited her if left to wander the Dreamland alone. "That's quite alarming. Maybe we should get you home before it comes back. It's a wonder you survived at all," I added as an afterthought. Not many could escape the Jabberwocky's clutches, from what I'd heard.

She shook her head, a frown marring the smooth brow. "No. Not before I find my sister."

I blew out an exasperated breath. *There's another empty-headed debutante running around the place?* The urge to leave them both to their fates nipped at the corner of my mind, but for once, taking the easy way out didn't make sense to me. I just couldn't leave this woman defenseless.

"Are you sure she's in here?" I asked, searching the periphery of my magical senses without encountering anyone else leaking their life-force indiscriminately. *No doubt she wandered in through a little-known portal and doesn't even realize it, while this sister is safely at home eating cake in front of the fireplace.*

"Well, no, I suppose not," she said thoughtfully, tapping her bottom lip with a well-manicured nail.

I snorted. "I certainly don't sense another person like you around here, so she's either back at your home, or dead." Her face fell, that bottom lip trembling under a manicured nail, and an odd panicky feeling flared in my heart at her distress. "Or maybe she's just too far away for me to sense her," I amended reassuringly.

The panicky feeling subsided as her lip firmed up, and she dropped her hands in front of her, clasping them demurely before pushing her chin into the air in a mildly defiant attitude. "Persi's not at home. She hasn't been for more than two years. But she can't be dead. Briar saw her. If I can find Briar, she'll help me find my sister." She lowered her voice conspiratorially. "I think there must be a path through the Dreamworld into the Wasteland, you know. That's where she was lost. I've never given up hope, and Briar's sure we can still save her—oh!" she broke off in surprise as her hands came up to frame her face, blinking rapidly as if seeing me for the first time. "I say! Are you—are you one of them?!" she asked, pointing to the gameboard next to her.

I turned to look at it, raising my eyebrows as I watched the little game pieces running around the square.

"Have you come to life to help me on my quest like a knight of old from Camelot?" I stared at her as she beamed at me, bouncing on her heels, her hands clasped in front of her chest. "And that would explain all this—" she gestured to me in general, still smiling like an idiot, "angelic beauty nonsense because you're a game piece with the virtue of a Knight of the Round Table. How lovely!" She practically squealed the last words, and it was my turn to blink at her, trying to process the nonsense coming out of her mouth. *How Wendy would laugh to hear me being compared to an angelic Knight of the Round Table.* "And I guess you're not a faerie after all! When you said you had faerie magic, you meant you were *created* with faerie magic, which explains the touchiness about not having wings," she continued with a firm nod.

I opened my mouth, but before I could correct her wildly inaccurate assumptions about me, she seized one of my hands, pressing it between both of her own. "I promise to return you to your game board once our quest is complete," she assured me solemnly. "But we must make haste. Briar said we didn't have much time to find Persi's whereabouts but the answers were here in the Dreamworld. Being a creation of the Dreamworld, you'd know better than anyone, wouldn't you? And you'd know how to avoid the Jabberwo—"

"Hush!" I shushed her harshly, putting my free hand over her mouth before she could say the vile creature's name. "You'll summon it if you're not careful. Names have power, don't you know? In here especially."

She looked abashed, so I dropped my hand away. "You're right, and I've been terribly rude and neglected to introduce myself. I'm Alice Eodor, Princess of Spindle—I'm not from here, I came through the dark mirror back there," she gestured vaguely behind her, but I didn't see any mirrors. She continued on cheerfully, "but please, call me Alice! All my friends do, and I'm determined that you and I shall be friends. As we're going on a quest together, we're bound to become close.

I pushed my fingertips onto my temples, kneading the sudden tension there. "Alice, I *just* told you names have power here. You shouldn't be giving me your name and title—we've only just met!"

"Oh," she replied, giving me a chastened look. "You did say that, didn't you? Except I didn't think my own White Knight would misuse it."

I sighed, putting my hands on my hips and not quite able to keep a half smile off my face at her innocence. "Well, I won't misuse it, but someone else could be listening, you know."

"You are quite correct," she agreed with a reassuring pat on my arm. "I promise to be more careful. I can see you will be very helpful. Well, Sir Knight, where to next?"

She turned to look around, and I felt oddly disappointed that she hadn't asked *my* name. I wouldn't have given it to her, of course, but for some reason, I wanted her to want it.

CHAPTER FIVE

Alice

With one last glance at the animated chess board where my companion had recently sprung from, I started moving purposefully toward the door that would lead to the ballroom. Now that I had a guide of sorts—though I didn't for one second believe he would stick with me for any length of time. People with those sorts of looks never did, and after all, he was a game piece come to life. Of course, he would want to explore—but before he wandered away, I hoped he could help shorten my search for Briar. Then I could find my sister, and all would be well.

The White Knight said something unintelligible behind me, but I ignored it in favor of the swelling music through the doorway. A sudden swirl of impulse hurried my feet, and I swept through the door, eager to see the dancers and perhaps join in for a dance or two. It seemed such a normal activity to be happening in such a strange world, and I wanted the comfort of it.

I caught a glimpse of whirling dancers in odd gowns and formal attire through the door before I was yanked back by my waist into the sitting room. I turned my head to frown at the White Knight. "Unhand me, sir," I ordered reprovingly, guessing he would respond quickest to old-fashioned, courtly language, given what he was. He dropped his hands, taking a step back with a sulky expression.

"I was only trying to prevent you from ruining your life," he defended himself stiffly. I couldn't help a burst of laughter escaping at the expression on his face. In his pure white knightly costume, it made him seem more like a boy playing dress-up, sulking at being caught with his hand in the cookie jar, than a powerful being of magic and dreams trying to protect a damsel. I rather liked his silly attitudes.

Still, the pout was threatening to turn into a thundercloud on his forehead, so I schooled my face into something like contrition. "I only wanted to see the dancers," I told him. "Maybe join in a dance or two. After all, I am dressed for a ball." I gestured to my gown, and he frowned at it.

"Yes, we will have to remedy that if you truly want to run around the Dreamworld. But take this as your first lesson on how to behave here—dancing in that ball without the proper precautions could have kept you there forever. Attracting the king's attention, or one bite of that food and—" he broke off, shaking his head.

"All right then," I said soothingly, pleased he was already trying to help. "Where *should* we go next? I admit that I haven't a clue as to where to start looking for Briar *or* my sister Persi."

"We can start by getting out of this horrible palace," the White Knight said, looking around for another door. I frowned at his insult to my lovely home—*not that this version of it is actually that lovely. It's so empty as to be menacing.* That thought made me forgive him for the slight, even if I still thought it undeserved—then I gestured toward a little door almost hidden behind a screen on the back wall.

"Let's go through that door there. It should lead to the servants' hall and an exit to one of the gardens. I won't be going out through the *front* door for love or money. It's where I left the Jab—I mean, the monster," I corrected myself quickly, remembering his instruction not to say the beast's name.

"How do *you* know where that leads?" the knight asked accusingly. It was hard not to smile again, as he did very much look like a boy who had the pleasure of his superior knowledge upset unexpectedly.

"Because I grew up here, of course. I know every inch of this *horrible* palace, as you called it," I replied with an angelic smile, knowing even from my brief experience how much it would irritate him. *That's a rather bad form for me, but it's too tempting to resist provoking that sulky pout.*

"Grew up here?!" he exclaimed. "Impossible. You forget I can feel how alive you are. You're not from this world," he said, his superiority re-established with that argument so much so that he looked down his aristocratic nose at me quite confidently, his arms crossed against the breastplate of his white armor.

"Not *this* version of the palace, no, but the real one. Or I suppose the one that's real in *my* world. An argument could be made that *this* version is the real one in *this* world, and *my* version is the fake one here, after all."

The knight blinked at me, clearly having *not* followed my train of thought. He abandoned it completely with a sudden shake of his head. "Never mind that. Let's go through the door and find the exit into the garden. With any luck, your sister and the other one—the one with the floral name—"

"Briar," I supplied with a grin, picturing Briar's reaction to *that* description of her.

"Yes, that one. With any luck, she and your sister will be sitting out there debating which flower in the garden is prettiest, and you can all go home before you're killed or worse."

It was my turn to blink at the knight. "Worse than killed?" I asked with equal parts delighted curiosity and real horror.

Instead of answering, he simply cast a dirty look in my direction and gestured for me to proceed him out the door. I obliged and swept through the doorway quite elegantly considering I had to manage my skirts and my blanket-cape, happily finding the expected servant's corridor beyond and following it to the door to the cutting garden as expected. When I reached out to grasp the doorknob, the White Knight caught my hand and pulled me back.

"Oh no, not so fast," he scolded. I pulled my hand from his and gave him a cool look.

"For a knight, you seem to need practice in chivalrous conduct," I admonished him. *Although if he was a game piece only a few minutes ago, maybe he's never had to practice chivalry. Usually, he'd spend his time bashing into other pieces to take them out of the game.* "Which is completely understandable," I rushed to reassure him. "Only please stop pulling me about so much."

The knight let out an exasperated puff of air. "I'm not pulling you around *that* much. Now hold still. I'm going to cover you in pixie dust so we don't have to worry about that blanket falling off your shoulders every five minutes."

Before I had time to blink, the knight had slipped his hand into what appeared to be a little satchel tied to a loop on his weapon belt and pulled out a handful of sparkling golden dust. With a few muttered words, he tossed it over me, blowing at the grains still sticking to his palm to make sure they all landed on me.

Unfortunately, his enthusiastic efforts meant that some of the dust landed directly in my eye. I blinked furiously for a few minutes, rubbing my itchy eye with my hand, even though I *knew* that would probably make it worse, and doing my best to stop the stream of complaints running through my head from exiting my mouth. *He's only trying to help, and if this works as well as he says it does, it will be worth it,* I told myself sternly.

I took a deep breath as the itching in my eye lessened, only to inhale what felt like the *entire* handful of pixie dust he had cast over me, and I promptly bent over in a choking, hacking cough. The White Knight's hand came down on my back, smacking between my shoulder blades firmly, tears streaming down my face—which, thankfully, cleared the last of the dust out of my eyes, though it wasn't the relief it might have been given the fact that I was now struggling to breathe—and after a moment, my coughs subsided.

I straightened up to find the knight looking at me with an expression somewhere between horror and disgust. I shot a disgruntled glare his way as I wiped my face, the remnants of my tears mixing with some of the dust and creating gritty tracks in their wake. I hadn't felt this grimy in years.

"What?" I challenged him, moderately embarrassed and wholly annoyed. *Surely he could have given me the dust in a more manageable way.* "We mortals have to worry about things like breathing and getting dust out of our eyes," I said tartly. "A magical being such as yourself wouldn't understand." I tried to act as if I still had some dignity left, but as his eyes started to crinkle in a suppressed smile, I gave up and laughed at the absurdity of it all. "Fine! I'm sure I looked absurd," I admitted, meeting one of his blinding grins with a rueful smile, "no one's perfect!"

He cocked an eyebrow. "At least your magic and life force should be hidden now. Although, if you carry on coughing and sneezing like that, any monsters on your tail will find you the old-fashioned way soon enough."

I scrunched my nose at him and only *just* refrained from sticking out my tongue. Instead, I turned to the door and pulled it open, not bothering to hold it for the *supposedly* chivalrous knight behind me.

In direct opposition to the shadowy palace we had just exited, the garden seemed even *more* alive than usual. I slowed my steps to gaze around in wonder. The colors were more vivid, the air denser, and the plants were huge.

"What a beautiful garden," I breathed as I looked around. "And you're simply enormous," I said to a gorgeous, brilliant orange tiger lily that stood even in height with me.

"And you're simply *rude*," the flower responded, seeming to peer down its nose at me, though it had neither nose nor eyes—nor a mouth to speak out of, come to think of it. "I'm exactly the height I should be, and if I had worse manners, I would remark upon how runty *you* are."

"I do beg your pardon," I responded immediately, my courtly training kicking in without thought. "I meant no disrespect at all. In fact, I was admiring your size—" the tiger-lily thrashed about irritably at my description— "I mean your majestic stature," I corrected myself, feeling the knight come up behind me. "And I didn't know flowers could talk," I explained, glancing down the flowerbed at the other giant flowers, who all seemed to have turned their attention toward us.

"Oh yes, of course we can," sighed a glorious pink rose, "only we usually wait to be spoken *to,* you know."

"No, I didn't know," I replied thoughtfully. "Although I don't think that's how it works in *my* world. I've spoken to many of the trees and flowers in this very garden growing up, and they've never answered back." I felt the knight shaking with laughter at my back, although he still didn't join the conversation. I elbowed him sharply without looking at him, but it only made him laugh harder.

"In *this* garden?" a purple violet the size of a hunting dog asked incredulously. "I've never seen you in my life. And I certainly wouldn't have ignored you if you had spoken to me. Manners indeed!"

"Oh, I'm sure you wouldn't have," I said soothingly. "I only meant in *my* garden, of course. The one at home."

"Well, there you are," a daisy said stridently, "why pretend you've come to *our* garden when you've only ever been in yours? Can't you keep things straight in your head?" she complained, triggering a swirling mass of complaints from the other daisies in the bed, who all twittered at once, causing a dreadful racket.

"Oh, now you've done it," the tiger lily complained, waving angrily at the daisies. "Once they've started, we won't have a moment's peace."

"I didn't realize!" I exclaimed regretfully, wondering how long it would take for the yellow and white flowers—which had hitherto been some of my favorites but were rapidly moving down the list in conjunction with the volume of their prattling—to settle down.

"They'll quiet down right now," the knight said threateningly, "or I'll pick every last one of them to make a bouquet for my lady here." The daisies gave a great cry all together, then fell silent.

"Oh, don't!" I whispered harshly, turning to frown at him. He only grinned mischievously, and I shook my head, turning back to the tiger lily in front of me. She seemed to be the one in charge of the flower bed.

"I do apologize; he didn't mean it," I assured her.

"On the contrary!" she exclaimed, casting an approving look at my companion, "Those daisies chatter on so noisily they only respond to threats. Not like the roses. *They're* even-tempered enough, but if you threaten them, they'll dish it right back," she said with a shudder. "Thorns, you know," she whispered by way of explanation.

"Well," I said, tapping my lip as I contemplated the matter, "one could always use gloves and gardening shears on the roses if it came to that."

A shuddering gasp ran through the flowerbed, and I blinked in alarm as the knight suppressed another laugh at my back. "Not that I *am* contemplating it," I added hastily.

"There's no need to flaunt weaponry," the tiger lily replied stiffly, and I found myself clutching my makeshift cloak around me as if it could hide me from scrutiny.

"Speaking of roses," the knight said finally, "we're looking for a Briar Rose. Have you seen any walking about? She would look more like milady here and less like one of the beautiful varieties in your bed," he explained gallantly.

A breathy twitter swept across the bed at his inquiry, and the flowers all giggled behind their leaves, fawning over him vapidly. I frowned at the silly things, then rolled my eyes as the knight bowed to them for good measure.

"We haven't seen a rose walking about, Sir Knight," the tiger lily told my knight indulgently, "but we *have* seen another who moves about the place like your lady. She comes through every now and again and drifts this way and that. Although, she's rather more like *you*, sir, with your lily-white coloring," she speculated, nodding at the knight's pure white armor.

"Oh!" I exclaimed excitedly. *That could very well be Briar— especially if they're mistaking the silvery threads of her dream-*

woven cloak as being white. Find her, and I can find my sister. A sudden fancy told me it could be Persinette dressed in white and wandering around, lost in the Dreamworld—further increasing my desire to find this person. "Has she been this way recently?! Only I *must* speak with her!"

"Indeed, she has, although she never has anything pleasant to say—only sobbing about things she's lost and such. Not like your young knight, here," she added. I drew on every bit of poise my governesses had instilled into me and refrained from snapping at the flower—*and* from elbowing the knight as he bowed in her direction again. *It's like a terrible pantomime where the actors have lost the script.*

"Perhaps my knight and I will be able to assist her then," I suggested to the tiger lily, who swayed thoughtfully. "Won't you tell me where she is?" I pleaded.

"*We* don't flit about the garden like seeds of cotton fluff," she said severely. "I certainly couldn't be expected to know *where* she is. I can only tell you she went *that* way last time she was here." The flower indicated down the aisle to our right, which stretched all the way to the inner bailey wall.

"Thank you very much," I said politely, then added a curtsy since they had all responded so well to the knight's bows. I felt him snort behind me and braved the flower's wrath enough to turn and glare at him. "*You* bowed at least twice," I accused, but only made his shoulders shake even more with suppressed laughter.

Tossing my hair over my shoulder, I swept regally down the garden path in the direction the tiger lily had indicated. Or as regally as one can while wearing an increasingly dirty ballgown and a blanket masquerading as a cloak.

CHAPTER SIX

Peter

"Do you really think it will be as easy as this to find your friend?" I asked Alice as she fluttered down the row of flowers, hiking her skirts up and snatching them away as a particularly curious rosebush reached out to snag them.

She whirled around at my question, her face rosy from exertion as she snatched her skirt away from the rosebush again.

"I don't know," she replied, exasperation evident in her tone. "But I do know that I won't be finding anything if I keep getting tripped up by these skirts! If only I'd have thought to change my clothes before riding off from the Academy last night, but it's too late now." The rosebush reached out from the flowerbed *again*, and even I was becoming annoyed despite the absurdity of the situation.

"Is that really necessary?" I asked it severely. "Can't you see that milady isn't used to tricksy flowers who have no concept of personal space?"

"Then she shouldn't be dangling her dress in my face," the flower answered back tartly, somehow managing to turn her nose up at us despite having no nose.

I laughed aloud at the flower's tone. "Fair enough!"

Alice screwed her face up in frustration. "If only I were

wearing a tea gown—or, better yet, my riding clothes! *Then* I wouldn't be bothered with all this nonsense."

I put my hands on my hips, considering the problem, then slowly felt my jaw go slack. There, in front of my eyes, Alice's clothes transformed seamlessly from a slightly dirty ballgown into a well-tailored set of fawn-colored breeches, a crisp white blouse, and a prettily embroidered sky-blue waistcoat. On her feet were tall, dark-brown riding boots, and on her head was a matching dark-brown helmet, the chin strap buckled tight. Oddly enough, she was still clutching the silvery makeshift cloak around her shoulders.

"Um, how did you do that?" I asked, reaching out with my magical senses but not encountering any telltale signs of spells or charms—or even a glamour. They always tasted like lilacs and baking powder in the back of my mouth, but there was no hint of any magical spells.

Alice's eyes flew open, and she gaped at her changed attire, her free hand reaching to pat her helmet. "I don't know!" she responded delightedly. "I pictured this exact outfit as I was wishing to change my clothes, and here it is!" She started fumbling with the clasp of her helmet with one hand, even as she continued to hold the blanket-cape in place with the other. I stepped forward, brushing her hand away to help with the clasp as she stared excitedly into my eyes.

"I suppose the helmet was a bit of overkill, and I wish the blanket had disappeared, but this will be *much* better for escaping the clutches of rogue roses and whatever else crops up here," she bounced on her toes in excitement as I struggled to get the clasp open.

"Do hold still," I told her, and she subsided with an apologetic grin.

I focused on the clasp, finally freeing it and pulling the helmet from her head. I considered her change in clothes a bit uneasily. Although I often changed my disguises—including the clothing I was currently wearing—while I was in the Dreamworld, it was a combination of prepared charms and glamours. She seemed to have conjured these articles from nowhere. *Could she be more powerful than I originally thought? But if so, why is she wandering around here with her head in the clouds? Surely she would understand the danger she's in.*

"Maybe the blanket didn't go anywhere because it's woven from dreams—it belongs here, you might say. And I suppose I was picturing the helmet when I was thinking of my riding clothes, so it came along for the ride, so to speak." Alice took the helmet from my hands, letting her cape fall from her shoulders and onto the ground as she refastened the clasp and looped her arm through the helmet strap.

"I suppose I should keep wearing the blanket," she continued forlornly, looking down at where it shimmered in the grass.

I huffed in annoyance and bent to pick it up. "You should probably continue wearing both the blanket *and* the helmet at the rate you're going. But neither is necessary since I gave you pixie dust." She watched me fold the blanket as small as I could, then tuck it into the satchel I carried at my waist, out of which I had pulled the pixie dust earlier. I stuffed it in, and Alice gaped.

"How can it fit in there?" she exclaimed, stepping closer and tugging the top of the satchel open to peer inside.

"Haven't you ever spelled a bag to be bigger on the inside than it is on the outside?" I laughed, letting her look for a moment before gently pushing her back and taking the helmet from her as well. I dropped it into my bag and pulled the drawstring closed again.

"No!" she exclaimed, curiosity lighting up her eyes. *Her very wide, very blue eyes.* I noticed. The shirt seemed to make them even lighter than they were earlier. *You could get lost in eyes like those.* They made me think of flying free through the sky on a sunny day, with adventures ahead and a soft bed to look forward to at the end of the day.

I gave myself a shake and took a further step back. "Well, never mind. They're common where I come from. And now you don't have to carry extra things. Shall we continue searching for your friend?"

She nodded, the light in her eyes dimming as her mission came back to her. "Come on," she said, waving for me to follow as she turned back down the path—neatly sidestepping the previously offending rosebush.

I bowed to the rose, which fluttered its leaves in response, and hurried to follow. After a few moments, I began to notice that the row of flowers—which we should have exited some time ago based on the length I had glimpsed when we were standing back with the tiger lily—wasn't getting any shorter.

"Alice, wait," I called, reaching forward to grab her shoulder. It felt slight under my hand, and I realized anew how vulnerable she was here.

She turned to look at me, breathing heavily as she brushed waves of blonde hair out of her face. "What is it?"

"The row of flowers," I replied, gesturing ahead of us. "We should have come to the end of it several minutes ago."

She blinked at me, then turned to look down the path ahead of us, hands on her hips. "I suppose you're right," she admitted, then motioned me forward. "Come on, let's run faster. Maybe if we're quick enough, we can get out of whatever problem area we're stuck inside."

I frowned in slight confusion at her words but followed as she began moving again. *Problem area?* I reached out with my magic to feel if any spells were keeping us trapped, but although there was plenty of the odd magic that was the fabric of the Dreamworld, there was nothing additional to it that I could sense. Finally, I tapped Alice's shoulder and motioned for her to stop.

"We still aren't getting anywhere," I said grimly. "I don't feel any spells in the area, so I don't understand why. Maybe we should go back the way we came?"

Alice, just nodded, bending down to try and to catch her breath. As she did so, I took a moment to look around the garden, pausing as I noticed a crumbling gap in the wall, that afforded a view down the valley spreading out in front of the castle. "Look," I said, pointing at the tumbled down breach. "What's—" I broke off as Alice stood back up, peering curiously at where I pointed. *Oh no. It's those underlings of the Jabberwocky. They're summoning him—or maybe they've just summoned him if she really did see him earlier.* Alice seemed entranced by their chanting, and I tugged at her sleeve.

"We have to go," I insisted, trying to control the nerves I felt at our current predicament. We needed to figure out a way to move, and scaring her *too* much wouldn't help.

"I would like to see the Jabberwocky for myself," she said, and I slapped my hand over her mouth. *Maybe she needs to be scared just a little.*

"Didn't I say you shouldn't even say his name?" I demanded in a frustrated whisper. "With how *brightly* you burn here, Alice, I'd bet he was lurking somewhere, just waiting to devour you. You need to have more care."

She seemed to be listening so I dropped my hand and took a step back.

"I certainly do have care, Sir Knight, but I take your point. Where, then, should we go? Will you still help me get out of here?"

I shuddered but nodded. "I promised to get you out and I will. But we must be cunning. There are worse things than the—" I mouthed *Jabberwocky* and just *knew* she was barely suppressing an eyeroll, then continued, "that will be attracted to all the *life* you're trailing everywhere. And I can't afford to lead them to my home either."

"Don't you live here?" she asked, glancing around the garden and back at the palace walls. I winced inside, realizing my little lie of omission about myself was becoming more awkward than funny.

"No, I—" the words explaining myself almost tumbled out of my mouth, but I stopped short, "No. My world is as different from this place as you could imagine."

"Is it very terrible then, your world, if you come here to seek refuge?" she asked, and I could see her thinking back to the chessboard I had saved her from touching, where she thought I lived. I stifled a laugh at the thoughts that were surely running through her mind, of a clashing neverending battle, and a knight who sought relief by growing larger and hopping out of the game. My almost smile faded before it began. Although I wasn't from that chess game, the analogy fit my life better than I wanted to admit.

"You would not find my world terrible." I said finally, answering her question. "And I will make sure you are safe." I cast a swift look through the gap at the chanting spellcasters and grabbed her hand. "Come on." I led us back at a walking pace toward the tiger lily. I was focused on her slowing breathing at first and didn't notice anything was amiss until Alice spoke.

"We aren't getting back this way either, it seems," she said solemnly, and we both stopped to stare at the path ahead of us.

It was true. We hadn't made any progress toward the original patch of flowers even though we had been walking for several minutes. *What is going on?* "I have never encountered anything like this in all my time in the Dreamworld," I said, but Alice didn't seem to be paying attention.

"We don't have time to be messing around," she was muttering to herself. "Although," she continued thoughtfully, her voice low as she tapped her bottom lip with her forefinger, "maybe that's the problem. It does feel a bit stubborn here, doesn't it? A bit like a child who is refusing cake because his brother got a bit with the blue icing, and there's only plain white icing left."

I glanced around, wondering *what on earth* she was talking about. There were no children nearby, and certainly no cake. Just endless flowers ignoring our existence.

"Yes, perhaps it's that," she said finally, her tone a little triumphant as she turned to me. "Let's begin again. Only this time, we'll walk toward the beginning of the row, and I'll try *very* hard simply to enjoy the view and *not* want to find the Lady in White so much." She stepped toward me, putting her hand on my forearm and leaning in confidentially. "I think I've irritated it by being more interested in *her* than in *it*, if you see what I mean."

I leaned closer as well, until our faces were only a few inches apart. Her words were absolute nonsense, of course, but the lively sparkle in her eyes made me want to tease her all the more. After all, I was along for an adventure—and if it was to be led by a mad young lady, I wanted to see just how mad she could be.

"Shall we fly then, Lady Alice?" I asked solemnly, and she frowned instantly.

"Don't be ridiculous," she ordered, giving her head a little shake.

I laughed, straightening up and giving her a superior look. "I'm not the one being ridiculous. We *could* fly, I'll have you know. It's one of the properties of the pixie dust I gave you," I revealed triumphantly. "Even those *without* wings can fly!"

"Well, obviously," she said patiently as if she was talking to a very slow child. "I couldn't help but sense *that* as I was choking half of it down my throat. But doing so *now* would only further irritate the Dreamworld. It wants to be helpful, you see. And I've been ignoring it completely, focused as I am on finding Briar and my sister. If we used *your* magic, it would only make things worse. Nobody likes to be shown up in their own home, so to speak. And I feel rather bad for ignoring it."

She said it so matter-of-factly, without any sense of superiority or lecturing tone, that I simply gaped at her.

"Are...are you saying that the Dreamworld has *feelings?*" I spluttered, crossing my arms over my bulky chest armor.

She gave me a puzzled look. "Of course. Can't you feel them? I would have thought *you'd* feel them more than I, considering you're a creation from the Dreamworld yourself."

I frowned a little uneasily. It had been a lark to let her think so at first, but now it felt a little bit like a silly prank gone bad.

"Oh, I am sorry if I've hurt your feelings," she rushed to assure me, misinterpreting the expression on my face and patting my shoulder in sympathy. "I'm sure you would be able to sense its feelings quite well if you wanted to. But such things wouldn't come in handy for a knight on a game board. Perhaps it's for the best."

She seized my hand and turned away as if leading a sulking child—albeit one several inches taller and with a good thirty pounds of muscle on her—and took in a deep breath. "On the count of three, let's run. I'll concentrate hard on *not* finding my sister, and you just keep up with me, and hopefully, it will all come right."

She gave my hand a tug and immediately began moving down the aisle.

CHAPTER SEVEN

Alice

As soon as we started moving, I forced myself not to think about my sister or Briar. Of course, that was impossibly hard, so instead, I began thinking very hard about the Dreamworld and the flowerbeds surrounding us, which was much more helpful for not thinking about my sister than thinking about not thinking of her. If that even made sense.

"I don't believe it," the knight murmured next to me. I glanced over at him, and he raised his eyebrows. "Your madcap idea seems to be working."

I glanced around and realized with delight that not only were we finally moving, we were moving in the opposite direction that we were walking. So instead of getting closer to the tiger lily we had spoken with earlier, we were actually leaving the row at the other end and turning a corner.

"Oh, *well* done," I told the Dreamworld enthusiastically, beaming around at it. I felt the fabric of the place perk up and preen, and in the next instant, we both cried out as we swept through something cold and a little clammy, and we stumbled to a stop. The knight proved his origins by pushing me behind him protectively and squaring up toward whatever we had walked through.

He needn't have done so, of course. It was clearly the

mysterious White Lady.

"I do beg your pardon," I called to her from around the knight's bulky shoulder. The Lady turned, and to my disappointment, it was not my sister, or even Briar, but it was undoubtedly the person the tiger lily had been speaking about. She was white from head to toe.

Not only was her floaty, old-fashioned gown pure white, but her hair was the lightest shade of blonde imaginable, and her skin was so white I wondered if she had ever seen the sun. She looked at us with mournful pale eyes, a slight frown forming between them as she blinked at us.

"Are you telling me we just walked through a *person*?!" the knight demanded. Before I could answer, he made a retching noise, and I swiftly backed away. He turned and emptied his stomach contents—which was curious, if also disgusting, as I didn't think game pieces would need to eat—and turned back to find both the White Lady and me watching him. "What?" he demanded defensively. "It's my first time walking through a person."

The White Lady turned her eyes toward me, and I shrugged. "I've never walked through a person either, but it felt exactly like walking through fog down by the river on a cold night, so it wasn't that bad. I trust we didn't hurt you?"

"It's more the principle of the thing than how it felt," the knight muttered as he stepped beside me, and I elbowed him sharply in a gap in his armor plates. For a knight, he seemed to be extremely chatty and a little over-sensitive.

The White Lady shook her head, her expression kind but sad. "You couldn't hurt me, child, do not fear."

"I take it this isn't your sister *or* your friend," the knight murmured, and I shook my head.

"You are looking for your sister?" the White Lady asked, and when I nodded, she took a step—or glided, perhaps, because she really did *seem* to be hovering over the ground instead of walking on it—closer. "I am looking for mine, too," she confided quietly. "Or rather, I know where she is, but I haven't been able to reach her."

"I am sorry to hear that," I said politely, and she tipped her head to the side, considering me.

"*You* might do," she murmured, then took my hand in hers. It felt very cool and smooth, but quite solid.

"I can feel you!" I exclaimed before I thought better of it.

She nodded. "Yes, I thought you might be able to—which is why you might be able to help me, if you're willing."

Her face was so filled with sorrow—the kind that bore its trace on every part of a person's body so as to weigh them down—that my heart felt quite heavy too.

"I should like to ease your burden," I told her, elbowing the knight again as he made a strangled noise of protest at my words, "but I am here to help rescue my sister. Perhaps you could help me find her, and once she's safe, the knight and I would be free to help you as well?"

"Your sister? Ah, yes, indeed. Come," she replied, turning on her heel and launching into a run so fast I almost lost my legs keeping up. Luckily, the knight had the reflexes of a cat and broke into a sprint, snagging my free hand. When I looked back to ensure he was okay, he grimaced at me.

"Don't give out favors to people without knowing who they are!" he scolded me. "If she was a Fae, she could take advantage of any thoughtlessly kind thing you said, and then you'd be stuck just because you were being polite!"

"She's not a fae," I told him confidently, though he only shook his head at me. Although I had never met a fae, seeing as how they had all disappeared at the same time as the long-ago Breaking and the formation of the Northern Wasteland, the woman's magic—though muted—seemed too familiar to be something so foreign. Not that I knew exactly *what* she was.

"Faster," the White Lady called back to us, "run as I do, and we'll soon be there!"

I tried to figure out what she meant, looking as closely as I could to see how she was taking her steps, but try as I might, I couldn't actually see if she was taking any steps at all under the long skirts of her gown. *I swear she's gliding over the ground.*

While I puzzled over this, we seemed to arrive at our destination. The White Lady stopped all at once, yanking my arm as I took a step or two forward, which had the unfortunate effect of slamming me backward into the knight and his shining white armored chest—an uncomfortable occurrence.

"Are you all right?" he asked as I disentangled myself from his arms. I nodded, then raised an eyebrow as he muttered, "Well, bully for you. *I* feel like I've had a cannonball shot at me from a yard away," and rubbed his chest with a grumpy expression.

"Not that you'd know what it actually felt like," I said pointedly.

"I've had that happen more often than you'd think," he muttered—more to himself. I raised an eyebrow. Although I was perfectly prepared to believe he knew what people crashing into him felt like—he was a chess piece, after all, that's how you took a piece off the board—there would be no reason he would have ever encountered a game piece shaped like a ship—especially one with working cannonballs. I opened my mouth to question him, but the White Lady distracted me.

"There," she interrupted, pointing off into the distance. I followed the direction of her hand and realized we were standing on a hill and could see for miles in every direction. "It's a thin space between worlds. Your sister is not there now, but she will be—she *may* be—soon."

I struggled to find the distant place she was pointing at but quickly realized that the more I focused on it, the clearer it became—as if the fog were clearing on a windowpane little by little. There was a sense that the world was laid out in a sort of pattern, and the feel of it hung around my mind until suddenly, I could see.

"It's laid out like a chessboard!" I exclaimed, the black and white squares suddenly visible even as the grass and forests and rivers were also completely solid and laid overtop the gameboard. It was like having double vision—both were in the same place at the same time.

"Indeed," the White Lady said, giving me a fond look. The knight leaned forward and frowned.

"I don't see a gameboard," he said grumpily.

I pointed to each square in turn, all laid out in wide rows. "See, the next row is over there—and the creek makes a sort of border to that row, so beyond it is the next one. If it were a real gameboard, we'd see the players lined up—why, yes, there *are* players down there. Maybe that's why *you* can't see it—I suppose you're one of them. What fun it would be to play in a game this big! I wish I could play—though I'd like to be a queen, obviously. She can move the best around the board."

"You may start as one of my players—one of my white pawns, you might say," the White Lady said regally. I turned and realized that she had a staggering crown on her head that looked both ancient and otherworldly. My grandmother had taller, more intricate ones, but the White Queen—for that was obviously who she was, though I hadn't seen it before—had one that fairly oozed raw power.

I dipped a curtsy at once. "I'm so sorry, your majesty. I can't think how I didn't recognize you before," I said humbly, then elbowed the knight on the way up. *He* should have recognized her, at least, and warned me.

She waved my curtsy away impatiently and gently took my hand. "You wouldn't have seen it before, my dear; it's only in recognizing the heart of the Dreamworld that you can see its players so clearly. You may take my daughter's place for now and be my pawn as you travel across the board below. I know you are eager to find your sister and your friend, but I must ask for your help. You are the only chance I've had in uncounted years—I am not always here, you know, after all. Mostly I'm scattered to the winds, unknowing and unknown, and always divorced from my body and soul. Only here, in the Dreamworld, can my spirit coalesce at times, and I remember what was forgotten."

The gravity of her words pulled at my heart. She seemed so fair and kind and *good* that I dearly wanted to help her. "Well, you're here now. Perhaps between the three of us, we could anchor you to your body with a spell of some sort. If you could tell—"

"No, no child," she interrupted. "This is not my body. I don't have enough time to tell my tale—only the end of it and the beginning of yours—if you are brave enough."

My fingers flexed in hers, which, although cool, felt real enough. *Perhaps she's mad. If she's lived here for countless ages, it would be enough to drive anyone mad.* I felt the knight step a little closer and put his warm hand on my shoulder—whether in support or warning, I didn't know.

She smiled as if she knew my thoughts and nodded to our joined hands. "Look, it begins already." I glanced down and was startled to see that her hand was transparent. I could feel its weight still, but a moment later, the entire thing had swirled away, and suddenly my hand collapsed around nothing, the weight of it gone.

"What—"

"Nevermind, child, but listen closely. The veil between worlds will thin in the place I showed you, across the board in the eighth row. It will be a difficult journey, but if you get there in time, the magic that lives in your blood will make you a queen, and you will come into your true power. When the portal opens, it will only open for a second, maybe two. Enough time to either jump into the other one or pull your sister into this one."

Excitement at recovering my sister warred with the distress I felt watching this wise and regal queen disintegrate in front of me. Only her upper body and face remained as she spoke now, floating eerily unsupported in the air.

"Though I know it will be a burden, I will ask it because I believe you can do it, and because it is right, and because it will reunite me with my daughter and husband, and because if you don't, we may never have a chance to conquer the evil that we missed in the first place." She drew in a breath and then blew it out quickly. "One of my sisters is here, chained against her will."

The disintegration was spreading up her chest now, and the queen spoke frantically, my heart beating faster as she drifted away, and I tried to understand what she was telling me.

"Red she is—as red as blood and steeped in blood—and only blood will free her. Follow the path and break her chains."

Only her face remained, and I still didn't understand how to find her or what to do. "What should I—"

"You'll know, my dear," the queen interrupted, only her smile and kind eyes remaining.

"How do you know?" I exclaimed.

"Why, I can sense my magic in you, of course, and hers—and something all your own. Have faith—and remember who you are!" she called out, then vanished completely, leaving my head a swirl of confusion.

Her magic? And her sister's too? A sudden suspicion of the White Queen's identity flitted through my head, and I turned to the White Knight, his warm presence behind me so at odds with the queen's cool, ethereal one. *He doesn't seem to be the same sort of being that she is. Nor does he have the feel of this place, either, as one would expect of a creature of the Dreamworld.* He can't have been a game piece from the game in the castle, I realized with sudden clarity. *So who is he, then?*

"Well, that was odd," he said, raising his eyebrow and giving me a nonchalant smirk. The slight tremor in his voice betrayed that he was as unsettled as I. "I suppose we should avoid this King. So which path do you choose? The way of the queen or the way to your sister?"

CHAPTER EIGHT

Peter

Alice looked at me with those wide, clear blue eyes. She seemed contemplative as she looked into my green ones. I shifted uneasily under her frank gaze. The business with the White Queen—obviously a powerful being and even now was causing me to wonder if she wasn't an incarnation of the White Queen—Lily's mother. I blinked, wondering if I had just been speaking to Lily's mother after a thousand years of her being lost. I could have told her news of Lily if I had known—it had to be her. She said she was searching for her daughter. If only I had been paying attention.

I cleared my throat uncomfortably, Alice's solemn gaze still watching me as if she was waiting for something. "I...I think that wasn't just a queen from a game board," I admitted, filling the silence between us.

Alice nodded, surprising me. "I think she was the spirit of one of the Shepherds," she said, tilting her head. "Do you know who they are?"

I scoffed. "Of course I know who the Shepherds are. Doesn't everyone?"

"I don't know. I wouldn't expect a game piece in the Dreamworld to know who they are." Her tone wasn't judgmental, but there was a challenge in her words. A part of me wanted to bluster, to continue to hide my identity so I could just play the White Knight, escorting a maiden on an adventure in the playground of the Dreamworld. But something told me the game we were playing had turned serious—maybe deadly serious—and although she might need a White Knight, she should know it wasn't me.

"I...I never said I was a game piece," I answered defensively.

She nodded again. "Yes, I suppose *I'm* the one who said it. You simply declined to correct me."

"Exactly!" I said triumphantly, but it felt hollow and silly. I hesitated, then added. "I'm not a knight, really. I was simply dressed as one for the masquerade. But then I found you and thought you might need some protection. You were bumbling around like an idiot—someone was sure to pounce sooner than later." I rushed on, more words tumbling from me awkwardly as she listened quietly. "And I'm happy to continue on your quest with you. Someone needs to make sure you don't accidentally wander into the Wild Hunt or something worse." It suddenly occurred to me that I had insulted her, and for some reason, I didn't like that, so I hurried to add, "Obviously, you're quite powerful if you can see the gameboard that the White Queen saw. I'm not saying you're not intelligent. Just that there are so many things that could go wrong, and everyone needs someone at their back on a quest. So I'll come along if you like. It's just... I'm not a trained knight."

"Hmm," was her only response to my speech, her grave look turning into a frown for a second before clearing. "I think the problem is that you *are* a White Knight, you just haven't discovered it yet."

I blinked at her, suddenly wondering if she *was* mad, but she turned around to look out over the side of the mountain, hands on her hips.

"To answer your earlier question, I don't know. I've been searching for my sister for so long—I can't give up on her. And I can't leave Briar alone here, either. If anything happened to her, my brother would be devastated." She turned to look at me over her shoulder. "They just got married, you know," she said conspiratorially, a saucy look crossing her face. "Literally an hour ago. The Sleep Fairy wed them by the ancient rites. Our parents don't even know yet. It was very romantic." She flashed a brilliant smile at me that scattered my thoughts for a moment. She turned away from me again, and they all came rushing back in.

"Wait, are you saying you have Faeries where you are from?" I demanded. She shook her head, still scanning the view in front of us.

"Not *Faeries* like in the old tales," she replied, repeating my slightly different pronunciation. "No one has wings or anything like that. But some of the old magic still remains in our country, and we give the title of Fairy to anyone who still has some of the old magic in their blood. The leaders of the seven main departments are given the title Head Fairy. The Sleep Fairy is named Cara. She's a bit abrasive, but she's good. I could see it even when she was scowling at us across the barrier at her cottage. I knew she'd help."

My shoulders slumped for a moment. I had hoped there was a community of Faeries still on the other side and that they could help tear down the barrier between Neverland and the old country. Still, it seemed like my Lady Alice had more help than I first assumed.

"So you're saying that your friend is old enough to be married and important enough to be married by someone as important as the Sleep Fairy?"

Alice turned around to look at me, her eyebrow raised. "Yes. She and Raleigh are both a couple years older than I am."

"And your sister, is she older than you too?" I asked.

"Yes," Alice said slowly, crossing her arms as a stubborn look entered her face. "She's seven years older than me."

I raised my eyebrows. "And didn't you say Briar came here to find a way to rescue your sister?"

"Yes," came the reply.

"So your sister has Briar looking for her, and Briar has a

husband looking after her. And I'm assuming this Sleep Fairy is still in the mix somewhere, since we *are* in the Dreamworld."

Alice frowned at me, her face almost sullen and her arms folded even more tightly across her chest. She looked so much like one of Wendy's kid brothers when they weren't getting their way that I could feel a smile stealing across my face.

Alice seemed to notice because she stamped one foot and demanded, "What exactly are you getting at?!" I couldn't believe how much the beautiful princess I was coming to know had transformed into a sulky child, and I didn't bother trying to stop the gust of laughter that burst from me.

My laughter startled her, and she stared at me with offended shock. I sobered up quickly, preparing to soothe her temper as I did with Wendy whenever I laughed at her. To my surprise, her sulky attitude gave way to a twisted smile, then an outright chuckle as she relaxed her arms, shrugging a little sheepishly.

"Sorry about that," she said with a grin. "I suppose I did look like a bit of a brat. I'm not *usually* prone to temper tantrums, but back home, I'm used to getting my way." She sobered. "Still, what you said is true. My sister and friend have others who either know where they are or are looking for them. And Briar said she knew that she would find my sister. But the White Queen seemed desperate, didn't she? It's so hard to know what to do. I wish there were a way to help everyone."

I swallowed hard, Alice's generous heart pricking my conscience. I had started all this by wanting an adventure and getting away from Wendy's nitpicking seriousness. And even a few minutes ago, when I pointed out she could abandon the search for her sister and friend, trusting that the others would find them—there was a part of me driven by my desire to see this thin place between worlds. To know if I could use it to join Neverland back to the old country. Even that desire—as altruistic as it seemed since I truly believe it's what Neverland needs—my biggest motivation was preventing my fate of becoming the Grand Pixie of Neverland after my mother passed. But here, Alice just wanted to help everyone. She wasn't thinking of herself at all. Obviously, since she's been blundering around half falling into traps and the clutches of powerful Dreamland beings.

I cleared my throat. "I think it's time I told you who I am," I admitted nervously, my habit of keeping my identity hidden warring with my desire to be honest with the person in front of me. A part of me knew she would never try to use me, never hurt me. The first time she had looked at me with those clear blue eyes, I could see her innocence and goodness. But years of experience made me doubt that such a person could exist. Still, I didn't want her questioning my motives for searching for the thin place later.

Alice didn't say anything. She simply gave me an encouraging look and waited patiently.

I took a deep breath and forced myself to speak. "I want you to take the White Queen's path and find the thin place because I could try to use it if you do. I've been trying to break the barrier between Neverland and the old country because I wouldn't have to become the Grand Pixie if that were gone. I wouldn't have to sacrifice myself for magic, and the humans could reconnect with their own people, and we could finally explore *something* that isn't our island or things made up here in the Dreamworld," I said, all in a rush. "Oh, and I'm a royal too," I added as an afterthought, then lowered my voice, "and my name is—"

"Wait, wait, wait," Alice interrupted, holding her hands up as if to stem the flow of my words and shaking her head. "You said Grand Pixie, right? As in the ancient rulers of Faerie?"

I nodded. "Yes, although after the sundering, it was renamed Neverland. We still call ourselves Faeries."

Alice took a steadying breath and then smiled. "No wonder you were so interested in the Sleep Fairy earlier. But we have no one in our world with powers like the ancient faeries—wait a minute, does that mean you *do* have wings?" she asked excitedly, wriggling like a puppy. "Oh no! I forgot it was rude to ask again!"

I nodded, an amused smile on my face.

"Can I see them?!" she demanded, clapping her hands and

literally jumping in place.

"No!" I exclaimed, a flush sweeping across my face.

"Oh please, *please*," she begged, fairly hopping closer and tugging on my arm, peering around me as if checking if I had freed them. "I would dearly love to see them. I bet they're wonderful!"

I shook her off, suddenly all too aware of her soft, warm touch and the scent of vanilla and orange that seemed to follow her around like a cloak. "No!" I said almost harshly, instantly regretting as a hurt expression flashed across her face, and she began to draw back and pull her enthusiasm inward again. I didn't want her to close off from me.

"No, don't—" I said, reaching out to grab her hand. "It's just that revealing your wings is a very personal thing." She stopped drawing away, but the hurt still lingered on her face. She didn't understand what I was saying. "I mean *very* personal. I don't even have mine yet—most faeries are born with them, but my family only seems to get them once you are bound to your spouse. Something to do with how we make the pixie magic, I suppose. At any rate, for our family, our wings are only ever seen by our spouses," I continued, and understanding flashed across her face, followed by a blush as bright as mine had probably been.

"Oh, I see! Oh no! I didn't mean to insinuate—not that you're not very attractive, obviously—but someone as handsome as you would already know that," she gulped as an amused smile crept onto my face. "Not that *I* think—that is, I wasn't trying to—oh dear." She finally stopped babbling and stared at me in embarrassed confusion, chewing on her lip. A part of me wanted her to continue, as I was *extremely* intrigued by the reference to my attractiveness. I couldn't help but puff out my chest a bit. She was adorably embarrassed, but strangely for me, I wanted to protect the vulnerability that hung in the air between us.

My name. I still hadn't given her my name! That would show her that I didn't mind her having a crush on me. *Not only don't I mind, but I want her to.*

Suddenly, I realized how badly I wanted her to have a crush on me—to depend on me to help her with her journey, whichever path she took. Something about this bit of dandelion fluff floating in the breeze had wormed her way right through my defenses. She was springtime after a hard winter. And I wanted that all for myself very badly.

But she didn't seem the type to try to ensnare my heart in return. She was a giver, not a taker. In fact, I only met her because she had rushed headlong into the Dreamworld to help her family, and the only reason she wasn't already doing so was because she was considering helping a third person—a virtual stranger—regain *her* family. *Alice would never reach out and take something for herself. She'll draw her desire inward and stuff it down until she can let it go.* I could almost see it happening as the blush subsided, and she tugged gently on her hand to disengage from mine. Instantly, I tightened my grip and tugged her sharply forward so she fell against me, steadying herself against my chest with her free hand.

"I didn't tell you my name yet," I said in a low voice, a flash of triumph flooding me as she gazed up at me—much closer this time—the flush spreading across her face in full force again. "It's Pe—"

"No, don't!" she exclaimed, wrenching out of my grasp and stumbling backward a step or two, putting her hands over her ears.

I blinked rapidly, hurt and confusion warring inside me. I had *wanted* to give her my name—to hear it from her lips when she spoke to me, but now she was rejecting me?

"Am I not good enough for a name, then?" I asked mockingly, balling my fists at my side. "You'd rather call me "Sir Knight" and remind me I'm only here at your beck and call to serve you on your quest?"

She looked at me in horror, shaking her head. "No, not at all. I would never treat someone—you certainly don't have to stay at my side. If you want to leave, then you *must* go. Please don't stay because you feel an obligation. Don't worry about me—I always land on my feet somehow." She laughed in a gentle, self-deprecating way that pierced my heart, proving what I had been thinking only moments ago. She was too giving. "It's quite the family joke at home," she continued ingenuously. "I get into all kinds of scrapes, but I always come out right. I know this place is dangerous, but I have faith that I'm here for a reason. And more than ever, I believe the Shepherds are watching out for me."

A dash of jealousy and determination flew through my heart. *I was right. She's trying to let me go now because she thinks it's what I want. She'd never admit if she wanted me to stay.* Little did she know that wild jabberwockies wouldn't pull me from her now—even if she simply wandered around the Dreamworld forever. And although her letting me go seemingly easily wounded me a little, it also lit a spark of challenge I was too happy to ignite.

"You can't get rid of me that easily, Alice. If you prefer me as your White Knight, I'm happy to be him. Only—" I couldn't help the vulnerability sounding in my voice, even as I tried and failed to keep the question I wanted to know from tumbling from my mouth. "Why don't you want to know my name?"

She must have seen the hurt in my eyes because she reached up and gave me a quick hug. "I *do* want to know your name—just not here, not now. You said names have power, and anyone could overhear it when you give it away here. I want to protect you. Besides," she continued, a playful grin overtaking her previously worried expression, "as much as you deny it, I think you really *are* a White Knight deep in your bones. Perhaps you should get used to being your true self for a little longer."

My mouth dropped open in astonishment as she grinned at me. *She's actually mad if she thinks I'm a White Knight. I'm as selfish as they come, and I don't regret it. Don't usually regret it*, I corrected myself. Still, it was nice to think that I could be a real White Knight in someone's eyes. And my heart warmed at the fact she wasn't taking my name right now in order to protect me.

Before she could pull away, I reached out, curling my knuckle under her chin and tipping her face up so I could look her squarely in the eye. A grin stretched my lips wide as I felt her erratic pulse beat under my finger. *She's not as unaffected by me as she wants to believe.* "I understand, Alice, and I thank you for your concern. But know this: I'll be giving you my name soon. There's no one I'd trust here more to keep it for me."

She shuddered delicately, then nodded, and I dropped my hand away. She stepped back, turning to look out at the view from the mountain again, and I grinned. *Definitely not as unaffected as she pretends.*

CHAPTER NINE

Alice

I stood looking off the mountain without really seeing anything, trying to get my traitorous heart back to a normal speed, the blush off my face, and the scent of honey and cinnamon that lingered around my knight out of my lungs. He had invaded all my senses, and his promise to tell me his name at some point seemed like a threat—a delicious threat.

Stop it, I ordered myself. *He's not doing it on purpose. People that look like him never are. Or they only half mean it if they are. Either way, it doesn't matter. He wants to help, and you need to make a choice.*

"We'll find the White Queen's sister," I announced finally, turning back to the knight and shrugging. "I don't know what path she was talking about following, but I assume it will become apparent once we start moving."

The knight gave me a sympathetic look. "I know you wanted to concentrate on your sister, but like you said before, let's have faith that it's the path we need to take."

Have faith—and remember who you are. The White Queen's words echoed in my head, but I shook them off. *Remember who I am? I'm still figuring out who I am. How can I **remember** it?*

"I suppose we should start running again," I said to my knight —*I have got to get out of the habit of calling him **my** knight. He's not.*

He's his own. And he's the type who would resent any appearance of clinginess. I know I would.

"Oh no, I don't think I can stomach all that nonsense again," he replied, stepping toward me and grasping my hand firmly. "I think we'll fly instead."

"Oh yes, the pixie dust!" I exclaimed and stepped off the mountain's edge, pulling the knight with me. I looked back to make sure he was alright and to check that I was doing it right—I was hovering a foot away from the edge of the mountain as I wanted to make sure I was using the pixie dust properly for a controlled descent instead of crashing into the brambles far below—and was in time to catch his startled expression before he covered it up.

I instantly felt a ping of remorse. *He had clearly been looking forward to teaching me how to use it.* I tugged on his hand and brought us back to the mountainside. "Would you like to show me how to use the pixie dust to fly?" I asked gently.

The knight crossed his arms. "You obviously don't need it," he said sulkily.

"Well, yes, it did seem rather intuitive," I agreed. "But you put the dust on me a while ago, and I've felt it settling into my bones and wrapping around my magic—*and* I've seen the Wind Fairy fly often enough that I can picture the difficulties in my head pretty easily. I'm sure *most* people would need *a lot* of instruction. It's a very good trick!" I reassured him.

"You have people who can fly in your world?!" he exclaimed.

"Just the most powerful of the Wind Fairies," I reassured him. "It takes a great deal of magic to be able to do it. I certainly can't on my own."

He still seemed inclined to sulkiness, and having felt the same myself more than a few times, I knew that further indulgence would just make it worse. "Come on," I said briskly, tugging one of his hands into mine again. "Let's get moving. Why don't you lead this time so I can see how a landing works? I'm sure I'll smash into a tree down below if I'm not careful."

He brightened at that thought and stepped confidently into

the air, tugging me with him gently. *If managing his ego takes this much effort, there's no way I could be with him.* I snorted, the sound snatched away by the air streaming around us. *Not that there's a chance for us—not that I* **want** *there to be a chance for us, no matter how much fun I'm having with him. Is this what a best friend feels like?* I shook my head. *What a waste of time these thoughts are!*

I focused instead on the ground rushing up beneath us. It should have been quite alarming, but the pleasant buzz of pixie magic was still wrapped around mine, and I realized that I *did* trust my knight—the knight, I reminded myself—to keep us both safe, so there wasn't much room for fear. It was too exhilarating.

Cold air pressed against us, plastering my clothes against my skin and whipping my hair into a frenzy. I was happy I had changed—*was changed the right term?* I wondered. *I hadn't changed my clothes in the usual way, one foot at a time and all that, but I had changed them by magic somehow, so I suppose it counts.* Regardless, I was thrilled to be rushing through the air in riding breeches instead of a flowing ballgown. In what seemed like no time, we slowed down to land gently in a patch of soft grass, which I managed to do right-side up instead of tumbling about.

"What is all this?" the knight asked, still grasping my hand as he looked around the meadow. I followed his gaze and instantly understood. A few yards away was a sturdy wooden platform, running along until it gave way to a quaint ticket office with a gabled roof. Along the platform lay tracked grooves, and I could just hear a bellow of steam being released from a whistle somewhere off in the woodland beyond the meadow.

"It's a carriage train platform!" I exclaimed in delight, tugging the knight toward the wooden platform and straining to look for the carriage train. "There's one in Dryfaeston that runs from the city center to a station near the forest. I rode it on the maiden journey. It was such fun!"

"What's a carriage?" the knight asked in a puzzled tone, followed up immediately with, "And what's a train?"

My mouth dropped open. "Don't you have carriages in Neverland?" He shook his head. "How do you get around then?" I demanded. "Just horses?"

He shook his head, a puzzled look on his face. "What's a horse?"

I gaped at him even more. "Fancy not knowing what a horse is! You don't *walk* everywhere, do you?"

He drew himself up with a scornful look. "Of *course* not," he replied, "we fly anywhere we don't want to walk—either by wings or pixie dust. And those without magic use boats to get around, or *yes*, they walk. They don't generally leave their harbor, anyway."

I shook my head in consternation as I tried to imagine a place where people could either walk or fly, but never ride a horse or carriage. The knight interrupted my reverie. "Tell me more about this carriage train. Do they have wings or some sort of spell that helps them hover off the ground? Do we take off from that platform?"

I laughed. "There's no flying involved at all. Come on." The knight moved with me willingly as I tugged him toward the platform, and we pointed down the rail, where it disappeared into the woods. "I can hear it coming, watch!"

I didn't immediately notice the other inhabitants of the platform, so excited as I was to see what a Dreamworld version of a carriage train would look like, until the knight nodded to someone off to our right. I turned to say hello, but the word caught in my throat as I caught sight of an enormous jewel-toned butterfly standing a few inches taller than me, its wings draped regally around its body. The knight huffed a laugh and used a finger under my chin to push my mouth closed, and I swallowed heavily, nodding deeply at the butterfly, who merely sniffed down its nose at me and leaned forward to try and catch sight of the train.

A quick glance around the platform revealed several more human-sized insects, including a bumblebee, a mayfly, and a bottle-green beetle. Out of everything I had seen and experienced so far in this world behind the dark mirror, these insects were probably the most shocking of all. Even more so than being hunted by the Jabberwocky or meeting the White Queen. Those sorts of momentous things could be expected in a Dreamworld—a place where anything could happen. But at this moment, seeing enormous insects dressed in three-piece suits and dresses waiting in orderly little groups for the carriage train to arrive, I did suddenly feel as if I really was having a strange dream. "Not a dream," I muttered.

"What's that?" the knight asked, tearing his boyishly excited gaze from the carriage tracks to peer at me.

"Just reminding myself that I'm *not* in a dream," I replied.

He frowned at me for a moment but was distracted as the steam engine carriage let out a great whistle and pulled into view. "Look at *that!*" he exclaimed. I couldn't help but grin in excitement too. "You're telling me these don't only exist here?!" he added in disbelief. "You have them in *your* world?!"

"Yes, we do. I'll take you on—" I stopped suddenly, staring at the side of his face as his eyes tracked the train's progress eagerly. For some reason, quite unconsciously, I had been expecting to show him around *my* world when this was all over. But could he even get to it? He had claimed the ballroom he stopped me from entering earlier was a slightly different plane of existence than this one, and for me to enter it would be disastrous. *But had that been because of the dance itself or because trying to enter a different plane of existence would be harmful?* I couldn't remember what he had said. Besides, I didn't even know how *I* could get back to my own world yet.

Unless I can find Cara's mirror again. Or if we make it to that thin place the White Queen mentioned. My heart, so light with the joys of flight and the carriage train's arrival, suddenly felt heavy as I realized that I might never share the wonders of Spindle with my new friend. I felt very low indeed.

The knight looked back to share his excitement at the train's arrival, but paused when he caught sight of my expression. "What's wrong?" he demanded immediately, turning his focus solely on me.

I shook my head. "Nothing," I said with a half smile. "Just, I would like to show you the train in Dryfaeston too, but I don't know if I ever can."

He understood in a flash, and I watched several emotions flit across his face in quick succession before his jaw firmed up in a stubborn line. "I would very much like to see it," he agreed, then added in a slightly more vulnerable tone, "and I would love to show you all over Neverland too."

My smile turned more genuine, and I couldn't help bouncing on my toes one or two times in excitement. *Surely we could find a way to explore each other's homelands. This is the Dreamworld, after all! Anything can happen!* Instead of saying anything more, we both turned toward the carriage train as it pulled to a stop and watched as a stream of insects and animals stepped down from their respective carriages and bustled around the platform.

"Shall we get on?" the knight asked excitedly as he stepped toward the carriage. He froze belatedly and held out his hand to help me across the gap instead of leaping into the carriage first.

"Yes, I suppose we should," I agreed, trying not to laugh at his eagerness. I'm sure I had been the same when the first one ran in Dryfaeston. "If nothing else, it will help us get across this row, and perhaps the carriage path is part of 'the path' the White Queen mentioned."

My knight merely bowed, so I took his hand and stepped lightly into the carriage, hesitating briefly as I surveyed the surprisingly spacious coach, which stretched further than I could make out in the gloomy interior. Not wanting to hold up the knight or any other travelers behind us, I quickly chose a seat next to a wooly sheep, and the knight took the space next to me. The sheep ignored us entirely, his nose stuck in a newspaper, but the mayfly seated opposite nodded regally, and the beetle next to it offered a polite "g'day," both of which I returned.

As the carriage train started forward, some of the knight's excitement returned. He was seated directly beside the outside door and leaned forward to look out the window. He leaned so far that I grabbed hold of the back of his chest armor to keep him from falling out. He pulled himself inside slightly enough to thank me, babbled something about the steam and sparks on the carriage line, and then stuck his head outside again. I kept hold of his armor just in case and smiled apologetically to the animals in the carriage.

"It's his first time riding a carriage train," I said to the car in general by way of explanation. Most of the animals nodded indulgently, although there were a few disparaging sniffs. The sheep seated next to me merely turned the page of his paper and ignored us all.

"Imagine hanging out of a window just to see the wheels on a track," a goat sitting beside the beetle said scathingly.

"He doesn't have carriages where he's from," I explained.

The goat merely looked down its nose. "Imagine that," he said to another goat, who was sitting on his other side in a floral print gown. "Living in a place with no carriages. Positively barbaric."

I frowned at them. "He said he flies to get around when he doesn't walk—which you or I wouldn't be able to do, you know!"

The goat raised its eyebrows. "*I* generally leave hard labor to the peasants, no matter what *you* might do. I certainly wouldn't be caught using my own wings to get around if I had any. Meaning no disrespect," he added to the mayfly seated across from me. The mayfly nodded to him regally but didn't add to the conversation.

"Don't pay any attention to these 'ere goats," the beetle remarked, shifting in its seat. "I use my wings to get around in a pinch, and I reckon 'e would too if 'e 'ad any. Your young man don't look like any breed of insect I've come across, but if 'e 'as wings, good on 'im."

"Oh, I don't think he has wings," I began, preparing to defend my knight even as a corner of my mind was bubbling with amusement at the fact that I was in a carriage train, verbally sparring with anthropomorphic animals regarding the childish conduct of a Faerie Knight. Thankfully, I was interrupted as the door between carriages opened, and a train conductor in the shape of a horse stepped through.

"Tickets, please," he neighed out, and a general fluttering arose as tickets were produced and the conductor began punching them.

"Oh dear," I said as he looked my way. "We don't have tickets," I explained. "Could you give us some?"

"Do you have any money to pay for them?" The conductor asked, and I shook my head. "Then how were you expecting to *get* a ticket? You must pay for one. Where are you going?"

I opened my mouth, but realized I didn't actually have an answer. "I don't know," I replied honestly, and the conductor snapped his teeth in obvious frustration.

"So you got on with no tickets and no destination?!" he demanded. Several of the other passengers began murmuring, the goats the loudest of the lot, *of course*.

"Fancy not knowing where you're going," the one in the dress murmured. "I'd believe anything of *those* two," the billy goat answered scathingly.

I tugged on the knight's armor, and he pulled back inside, his cheeks bright red behind his helm and his eyes shining in excited exultation.

"They're asking for tickets, but I don't have any money, and I don't know any of the stations!"

"What's money?" he asked, not disturbed in the least. I gaped like a fish and turned back to the conductor.

"Well, you should have said," the conductor scolded me severely. "If you've brought security, of course, we wouldn't charge you—for however long you're riding."

"I wouldn't call *him* security," the billy goat said, but the conductor merely shushed him.

"He has armor and a sword, doesn't he? You'll call him anything he likes if we come across the Wild Hunt. He'll be your only defense if they try to break into your car."

With that enigmatic remark, he swept out of the carriage door and into the next one to continue collecting tickets.

"I didn't need a ticket to ride the carriage train where I'm from," I explained to the sympathetic beetle, unable to help myself from trying to keep the good opinion of *someone* in our coach.

"You don't seem to know much of *anything*," the mayfly finally said, as the knight stuck his head—and only his head this time, thankfully, instead of hanging half out of the window—back outside. Thus rebuked, I settled back into my seat, watching the scenery go by and wondering what the Wild Hunt might be.

CHAPTER TEN

Peter

A carriage train. It was a revelation. And Alice says she has them in her world. It seemed to run on magic—at least, I felt some sort of contained spell in the engine at the front of the line of carriages, but it was a very small sort of magic considering how large the train was.

Is it a large spell that's been shielded, or is it truly a tiny spell? We had nothing like that on Neverland, relying instead on pixie dust to provide any convenience we could want.

I dipped my head back into the carriage every so often to check on Alice, but everyone seemed to be behaving themselves, and Alice didn't seem to share my enthusiasm, so I felt happy to enjoy the new experience my own way. After some time, we crossed a bridge over one of the streams that Alice said separated each row of the chessboard and slowed to a stop next to another platform like the one we used to enter the train.

"We'll have to get off here," Alice said when I pulled my head back in through the window. "They're saying it's the end of the line."

"Can't expect the train to go through the Woods of Forgetting," a billy goat said in an exasperated tone as he swept by us. "The driver would forget what he was doing, and then where would we all be?"

"In the Woods of Forgetting, presumably," I muttered under my breath, drawing an angry gaze from the billy goat and a startled chuckle from Alice. I puffed my chest out in pride. She really was a fun companion. I liked making her laugh.

We all piled out of the carriage, and as the animals streamed around us, confident of their destinations, I turned to Alice. "Any idea how to get to the next row?" I asked.

"If I remember correctly from the top of the hill, it's that way," she said, pointing toward the forest that the billy goat had named the Woods of Forgetting.

"Then I suppose we'll have to go on foot," I replied. "Or I can try to fly us."

"I wouldn't suggest it," said a voice near my elbow. I turned to find a dapper little gnat dressed in bright green and yellow. "You'll forget how to do it and crash. I did it myself when I was a young lad."

"Thank you for the tip," I told the fellow gratefully. "How can we get through, then? Is there a way?"

"Oh yes, there's a way," he said encouragingly. "See, the track starts over there. If you stay on it, it will lead you directly through the woods. As long as you start on the track, your feet will generally lead you through to the other side. The trick is not to get distracted by the rockinghorse flies or bread-and-butterflies. They do tend to lead travelers astray."

I wrinkled my forehead as Alice exclaimed, "What's a rockinghorse fly? That sounds lovely!"

The gnat drew itself up as if offended. "No more lovely than any other insect, I assure you. And much more of a nuisance."

I shook the gnat's hand appreciatively. "She meant no harm, good sir. Only I don't think she has rockinghorse flies where she comes from. Thank you for your help."

The gnat tipped his hat to me and cast another offended look at Alice. "Mind you don't stray from the path. They all look innocent enough, but you'll forget to eat before long, and then your number will be up!"

He walked off, and I grabbed Alice's hand to lead her toward the woods. "Speaking of 'following the path,' I think this one's clear enough—don't you?"

"I don't see how it could be any more clear," she replied with a smile that soon drooped as we clattered down the platform steps together. "I didn't mean to insult that gnat. I feel quite bad about it. Do you suppose I should go find him and apologize?"

I shook my head. "I'm not sure any of these people are real, living as they do in the Dreamworld, so I don't think manners matter very much here."

Alice rolled her eyes. "Manners matter everywhere. Besides, I thought *you* were a creature of the Dreamworld at first. Should I have been rude to you?"

I grinned and swung our hands between us. "I didn't say you had to be *rude* to them, just don't mind so much about manners. And I would have *loved* for you to be rude to me. I invite you to try your best now."

Alice rolled her eyes again but grinned as well before focusing back on the rapidly approaching woodland. "I admit, I'm nervous about these woods. Will you help me remember who I am? And what we're doing? I shouldn't like to forget my own name," she muttered to herself at the end.

"I've never been in these woods," I admitted, shrugging my shoulders. "I can't make promises. But maybe my pixie dust will help," I added with a reassuring squeeze of her hand when she started nibbling on her lip nervously. She pulled a little closer to me—close enough I could feel the warmth rolling off of her—and we stepped across the wood line together.

I had expected an immediate reaction as we crossed the wood line—an instant effect of whatever spell made people forget—but there was nothing.

Very much nothing, actually. The forest was silent, save for the faint scrape and thump of our feet on the little dirt path we were walking on and a pretty sort of whispering that was almost inaudible. *It must be the wind in the trees, though I've never heard it so melodic.* Otherwise, there were no other sounds. No birds fluttering, no squirrels scrabbling.

Alice stayed close to me, and I was grateful. For some reason, the feel of the woodland unsettled me greatly. I had never been to this part of the Dreamland before. Or at least, I couldn't remember being here before. It was nothing like the raucous jungle I was used to in Never...Never something. *The place. With the—the people, and the stuff that helps us do things.* It was confusing to think about that place. And what was it that we did? Something. There was something there that helped us with everything, but I had the sense that I didn't like it, whatever *it* was.

"It's very confusing in my head just now," I remarked aloud as I plod along, then startled as a voice next to me answered.

"Why, I was thinking the same!" it said. I looked over to find I was holding the hand of a beautiful young woman, who was looking at me with a sort of mild confusion. We both trailed to a stop and turned to face one another.

"Who are *you*?" I asked in pleased awe.

"I...I'm—well, I know I *have* a name, but I can't think what it is right now," the beautiful woman replied, her brow wrinkling. She blinked at me, her lovely blue eyes reminding me of something, though I couldn't think what it might be. "Do *you* have a name?" she asked.

I puzzled about that for a moment, then shrugged. "That's a good question. I rather think I do, but I haven't the first clue what it might be."

"What a curious problem," she said, then looked at our joined hands. "I seem to recall that I shouldn't be holding hands with someone I don't know," she said doubtfully. "Though I can't remember why."

I frowned at our hands as well. I was reluctant to let go of her hand—delicate and warm in mine. Although I couldn't think of the woman's name, I felt *very* strongly that I wanted her with me. Especially if I kept on forgetting things.

"Well, it's true that we don't know each other's names, but I'm not sure that means we don't *know* each other," I told her, warming to the idea as I spoke. "After all, I'd give you my name if

I had it just now, only I don't. So it's not as if I'm trying to keep it from you."

"Well, that's a good point," she replied thoughtfully. "And I do feel as though I know you, though I can't think why since I've never seen you before. You're dressed as a...." she gestured with her free hand at my clothing, and I looked down in surprise to find that I was wearing a set of hard white things that had a fancy design traced in a lighter shade of white, "a thingummy," she finished lamely, giving me a sheepish smile.

"I don't know why I'm wearing this," I admitted. "It's very uncomfortable; I'll have you know. I'd much rather wear what you have on," I replied, gesturing to the softer-looking clothing she sported. "It looks much better for racing about and climbing these...." It was my turn to wave my free hand around as I gestured to the large things surrounding us just off the path where we stood. "By golly! I just remembered one thing! We're standing on a path!" I proclaimed triumphantly.

The woman looked down and then back up at me with approval. "I believe you're right! Well done, indeed. It *is* a path. Can you remember why we're on it, though? I can't. However, I feel as though we should stay on it."

I shook my head. "Not a clue as to why we're on it. Though I agree we should stay on the path, seeing as how we know what it is. As tempting as those," I waved at the large objects just off the path again, "*things* are—and by George, I do want to scale one and see what's fluttering around the top with those tiny wings—we should probably keep to the path. Do you *mind* if we keep holding hands? I would like that above anything."

"Oh, we certainly should keep together. I find I don't want to let you go now that I've got you with me. I think we'll both do better together."

"I agree. You seem to be a good sort, and I'll wager you're great fun when it comes to an adventure. Just the type I'd like by my side."

"Well, thank you," the young woman replied politely, beaming at me and taking my other hand. "I can tell you're a good sort too. It's nice the way your heart shines all golden like that," she said, tipping her head toward my chest. I glanced down but didn't see anything and shrugged as she continued speaking, "But somehow, I don't think I'm the type of person who goes on many adventures."

"Nonsense," I replied stoutly. "What would you call this?"

She looked doubtful.

"Maybe you just can't see yourself very well in that regard." I looked down at my chest. "I can't exactly see my heart shining out. Maybe we aren't able to see those parts of ourselves. Because you have the spirit of adventure making music around you," I listened to the swirling notes that were only faintly audible. "Can't you hear it?"

The woman shook her head but smiled. "What does it sound like?" she asked. "Your heart is all shifting gold and green. It's beautiful."

I blinked at the expanse of white across my chest, wishing I could see what she saw instead. I liked the idea of a shining heart. I couldn't help puffing out my chest.

"You sound like a great wind in the ... the whatsits," I answered, tugging one of my hands out of hers and gesturing around at the large things growing off the path. "Or like the sound of huge swelling waves on a sunny day at sea."

"What's the sea?" she asked excitedly, bouncing on her toes.

"I don't know," I answered honestly. "Except it sounds just like you!"

"Oh, I like that," she replied. "We should go find it together! Then we'd know what it was like!"

We stood grinning at each other for a long minute when a sudden crash broke our otherwise quiet surroundings. A shape tumbled out of the gloom—a brown-furred animal with white spots on its back, looking at us with large eyes. We all stood as still as stones, staring at one another. After a charged moment, it dashed down the path and was soon out of sight.

"I have a feeling we should be going that way too," I told the woman next to me firmly. I longed to keep her safe with me, and going down the path felt like the best thing to do.

"Yes," she replied thoughtfully. "That does seem the thing to do."

I tucked her arm under mine, and when she reached up to hold onto me with her other hand, I pressed mine on top, keeping her securely anchored to me in case anything else came dashing across the path.

We walked steadily, the sunlight reaching us in dribs and drabs through the branches, though we never caught sight of the fawn again. Finally, the trees began to thin, and I could see a stream babbling away ahead, cutting right across the path Alice and I walked on.

I stopped with a start and looked over at her. "I've just remembered your name," I said, awareness of who she was and who I was rushing in around me all at once. Shame coursed through me as I remembered her description of my shining heart. *That was as wrong as can be. Anyone who knows me knows my heart is small and black, not glowing with sunshine.* Still, a wisping wish curled around my chest that I *did* have a shining heart.

Alice seemed to read something of my thoughts in my face based on the empathy tracing lines in her expression. She squeezed my arm and opened her mouth, making me cringe away at the sympathy I expected to drip from her words, but she stopped, a startled expression on her face.

"I still don't know your name," she said in bewilderment.

My heart wilted even further, remembering that I had kept it from her originally, and then she had stopped me from telling her later on. *Seems fitting,* I thought bitterly. *I was a White Knight back then. But now she needs to know who I really am.*

"It's Peter," I said roughly, almost glaring down at her, "Peter Pan."

"Peter Pan," she repeated quietly, as if tasting the words and finding them pleasing. The sight made my heart sing, and I shuddered, using the motion to pull away from her.

"Come on," I called over my shoulder, stalking toward the

stream. "I told you'd I get you to the other side of the woods if I could. You can't say I didn't uphold my promise." I jumped over the stream, then hesitated. *It was a long jump, and she's a bit smaller.* Despite the irritation swirling in my chest, I stepped into the water, my white metal boots keeping my feet dry, and held my hand out to help her. She took it with all the grace of a true princess, her expression gentle and the color on her cheeks modestly high. I could just imagine her sweeping up the skirts of a beautiful gossamer gown like the faerie ladies wore during the midsummer dances as she leaped with the grace of a deer and touched down lightly beside me. My heart ached to see her dance the equinox dances under the moon. *It would be a sight worth seeing.*

"Thank you, Peter," she murmured softly, and my heart turned in my chest. I had to admit, she had wormed her way firmly into my heart. I knew without a doubt I wanted her forever. And I hated it.

CHAPTER ELEVEN

Alice

I took the hand Peter offered to assist my crossing of the stream with embarrassment and a tinge of shame I was sure betrayed itself on my cheeks. His words from the woods haunted me, flitting around my ears as if I could still hear him speaking. You have the spirit of adventure making music all around you.

Obviously not, since he thought I was so delicate as to require assistance to cross a stream no larger than the one at the bottom of the garden in the summer palace. My only adventures, besides the one I was on now, consisted of attending balls and helping those in need. Even this adventure behind the dark mirror began as a desire to help Briar find my sister. *And now I'm on a mission to help one of the Shepherds. If not for those duties, I would be back at the capitol attending court or something else pleasant but dull. And that's exactly it. There's always duty behind everything we do—a happy duty of love for family and country—but duty all the same. I've never been adventurous in my life.* Peter must have been seeing *himself* reflected in me, not the real me.

Peter Pan. I glanced up at the man beside me as he let go of my hand, stonily pushing forward—*dare I say stomping*, I thought with a fleeting smile at the hints of childishness that often popped out in his conduct—as the path continued toward another woodland. I finally knew his name, and it suited him to the core. Peter—at least in my country—meant trusty as a rock. And Pan evoked the myths of the ancient fae who helped the Red Queen manage the wild land and growing life.

A ghost of the image I had seen in the woods still hovered around Peter, his heart glowing from his chest as he led us forward. He was, in truth, a White Knight, though his white light was dashed with the warmth of the sun and the green of life. He wasn't the type of truth seeker who would sit in a tower and only think. He was the type of person who would dive headfirst into everything life could offer. I thought back to my first impression of him. Even then, I thought he had the heart of a White Knight, but that somewhere along the line, his responsibilities had convinced him he'd never be able to live fully. He had great potential, but he was letting sorrow shutter his light. I wished I could stay and adventure with him always. I knew I could help him with whatever sorrows he bore. *But would he ever want someone like me? He'd be bored in a month.*

Peter glanced back at me and scowled at whatever expression he saw on my face. *He's smarting as much as I am from what happened in the woods.*

"There's a sign ahead, though I can't make sense of it," he said sullenly. I repressed the urge to grab his hand again and instead took a few quick steps until I was alongside him. The road split in front of us, each branch leading into equally dark recesses of the woods around us. A signpost stood where the road split, and on top were posted two signs. Both said, "Messrs. Tweedledum and Tweedledee," and each pointed in opposite directions.

"They're the same sign," Peter said, "but they point in opposite directions. Which way should we go?"

I considered the question for a moment, then shrugged. "If we take the signs at face value, I suppose it doesn't matter. Either path will lead to the same destination."

Peter let out a begrudging chuckle. "I suppose you're right. Which path do you fancy?"

I gave him a timid smile. "This one?" I asked, pointing to the one on the right, which *felt* better somehow although it looked the same.

"Right-oh then," Peter agreed, then started off, seizing my hand, seemingly without thinking, dragging me along behind him. He paused momentarily when he realized what he was doing, but since he had made an opening, I wasn't about to let him get away again.

"Come on," I urged, tugging him forward now, and he acquiesced without a fuss.

We walked for ages, often coming to little forks in the path that all looked the same. We took whichever fork felt best and continued on. Peter soon tired of the monotony, though he made a valiant attempt to hide his temper. I did, too, and before long, we were both dragging our feet down the path, mumbling complaints to ourselves and each other if only to pass the time.

Finally, we came to one that felt final somehow, and I pointed to the right-hand fork. "It's that way," I told Peter, then prevaricated a little, "At least, that's the way to Messrs. Tweedledum and Tweedledee. I don't know if it's the way out of the woods. But perhaps they'll tell us, if they're at home."

"I'll make them tell us," Peter muttered sulkily, so I poked him and continued on.

We quickly came upon a ramshackle sort of homestead, which looked as if it would be happier tumbled to the ground but stayed upright out of sheer spite. There was an open-air smithy on one side, with a roaring fire though no one was working it at the moment. Not far away were several storehouses and little sheds. A house stood on the other side, though it was a very strange house. The woodland hadn't been cleared for any of these buildings, and the house and the others seemed to have been built around them, but quite poorly.

"I should think it leaks dreadfully when it rains," I whispered to Peter.

Before he could respond, a doleful voice rang out. "It's rude to criticize someone's house, especially right in front of them."

I jumped and couldn't help myself from clutching Peter's

hand tightly.

"I'm very sorry—" I began, my eyes darting between the two young men standing off to our right, who I had somehow missed earlier. They stood each with an arm around the other and had such snide looks on their faces that I felt a sliver of dread in my belly at the likelihood of their helping us. Before I could make a proper apology, Peter interrupted.

"She wasn't being rude, only telling the truth, as anyone who has eyes can see." I elbowed him again, but he ignored me, giving the two young men a challenging look.

"Some might have eyes but not be able to see," said one of the brothers, for brothers they clearly were, and their identical faces marked them as twins.

Peter opened his mouth with some witty retort, but I jumped in before he could insult them further. "A fair point," I said in a conciliatory tone and elbowed Peter again. "And I do apologize for any hard feelings I've caused."

"Hard feelings?" Dee scoffed, for I had just noticed their names were embroidered on the leather aprons they both wore. "Feelings are soft, as anyone would know. And we haven't had feelings in years."

"Decades, even, if you want to be more precise," Dum added, then removed his arm from around his brother's shoulders. "Come on, Dee, we can't stand around chattering all day. We have work to do."

"You say that as if *I* don't know. I'm older—I've been doing work longer than you have."

"Being five minutes older, I don't think it counts as much of an advantage. But I'm taller, and that *does* count."

"Not in smithing, nor in anything else we do," Dum said in a superior tone as they turned toward the smithy.

"Oh, please!" I cried out in desperation, "Won't you help? We're only looking for a way out of this wood. We want to get to the fifth row as soon as we can."

"The *fifth* row?" Dee said scathingly, even as Dum shushed me loudly.

"Do be quiet," he said severely, twitching his neck to point using his head somewhere off to our left, "or you'll wake *him* up, and then we'll all be having it!"

I peered around Peter to see a man sleeping, propped up against a tree not far off. His clothing was unremarkable except for its decrepit condition, and his body was marked in faded tattoos interrupted by scars and fresh wounds alike. His hair was a sort of tangled mousy brown. On top of his head was a crown made of woven twigs—rustic but somehow noble as well. His unlined face seemed haunted as he twitched in some nightmare, and although he didn't look old, he didn't seem young either.

"He needs help!" I exclaimed, starting to move toward the man. Peter held me back, and I looked at him in consternation. He shook his head.

"We don't know who he is—except that he's powerful. Can't you feel his magic from here?"

Dee cackled at Peter's words. "Listen to your man, little oyster. He knows what he's about."

I blinked at the odd endearment, then scowled at them all. "Even if he's powerful, he obviously needs help. Look at his wounds!"

"*Don't* look at his wounds," Dum countered snidely, "especially if you're as silly as to want to help him because of them."

"Wake him, and where do you think *you'll* be?" demanded Dee rudely.

I felt Peter draw me back against his chest, switching his hold from my hand to my shoulder, but I couldn't help volleying back to Dee, "Right here, obviously, helping someone in need!"

"No, indeed," he cackled back, "you'll be nowhere! That's the Red King, over there, or what's left of him when he *is* the Red King. And what do you think he's dreaming of?"

I shook my head. "How would I know? Nothing good, at any rate, by the way he's whimpering."

"Well, you've got that part right at least," Dee shot

back triumphantly. "He's certainly dreaming of something unpleasant. He's dreaming of *you!*"

"How could he be dreaming of me?" I demanded, "He hasn't even seen me."

"I know he's dreaming of you because you're standing in front of me now," came the answer. "You wouldn't be here if he were awake. You're just a figment of his dream!"

"Well," I retorted angrily, "wouldn't he be dreaming of all of us if I were merely a figment of his dream?"

"How do you think any of us are here if not from the dreams of the likes of *them?*" Dum interjected waspishly. "But, *we're* not stupid enough to wake him while he's here, even if *you* are. He often goes there to nap when he's human enough to need a nap, which happens less and less through the years. Isn't that right, brother?"

Dee nodded wisely. "It's because *she's* nearby, of course, his Red Queen—though he doesn't realize it. If he didn't give in so much to his *other* form," nodding significantly at me and Peter as if we knew what he was talking about, "maybe he'd find a way to her at last."

"Of course, he wouldn't," Dum cried scornfully. "The other queen is too powerful to let them come together again. They don't hold a candle to *her*," he added, then marched off toward the forge, his brother trailing behind.

I looked up at Peter, who was clutching me back against his chest and frowning as they stomped away.

"Whatever do they mean?" I asked, bewildered. "What other form? And if that's truly the Red King, maybe we should wake him. He obviously wants to find his wife, and it looks like these two know where to look."

Peter shook his head and looked at me. "Ignore them, they're only talking nonsense. As for the other one—" he glanced at the king then back at me. "If it's truly the Red King, then I don't think we should wake him. The White Queen didn't mention him in her instructions, and he's not pointing to a path." He hesitated a moment and gave me an uneasy look. "There's something about him that makes me want to leave him alone."

I cast another glance at the humble-looking king. It almost hurt to leave a being like that without offering aid, but I could hear the wisdom in Peter's words. The Dreamworld hadn't been too dangerous since I'd been with him, and ignoring his advice now would be dangerous.

Peter seemed to sense my turmoil because he wrapped his arms around me and squeezed, hugging me from behind and resting his chin on the top of my head briefly before letting me go and snagging my hand again. The sudden show of affection bewildered me. I wasn't the type of person who invited physical affection, but I missed the warmth of his embrace as soon as it had ended.

"Let's go see if those two idiots will help us one more time, and if not, we'll find our own way," Peter said confidently, and we started toward the forge.

They were busily at by now, with stacks of shields and bits and pieces of metal that I was beginning to recognize as armor the closer we got.

"Why, I think it's almost nighttime," I remarked to Peter. It seemed to be darker, and although the woods were dim, it felt more like an evening dimness than a cloudy day dimness. *Does it have night and day here?* I hadn't noticed a sun traversing the gloomy sky, and now that I thought of it, I had no idea how much time had passed since I entered.

The Dreamworld had been an elusive presence around me since I arrived through the mirror, sometimes almost sentient, other times merely quiescent. Back in the garden, it had clearly wanted my attention, having felt almost jealous that I was focused elsewhere. Here it felt menacing and ominous, a very different sort of place to the wonders of the carriage train or even the strangeness of the mirror castle.

A stiff breeze blew up. The twins yelped and began rushing around their forge, banking their fire and shoving tools into little alcoves. I turned to glance at the sky—or where the sky would be, if we were back in Spindle—but all I saw was a raven descending, beating its wings to control its descent.

"I think that bird is causing the wind," Peter howled in my ear over the rushing noise. As it descended, the bird cawed noisily, growing larger the closer it came.

"Wait—" I said, hearing the note of panic in my voice, "it's not just larger because it's closer, it's *actually* getting larger!"

"Run!" Peter yelled, all of our thoughts of the Red King and the path out of the woods forgotten as we dashed away.

CHAPTER TWELVE

Peter

The raven flying toward us fairly dripped magic and was large enough to block out the light. I kept Alice in front of me as we ran between the trees, far off the path now.

"Here's someone's scarf blown away!" Alice exclaimed, reaching for a filthy rag of faded red as it swept by us. I recognized it as part of the Red King's garb and almost pulled her away, but she snatched it before I had the chance, and a second later, we were tumbling into a sunny meadow. The wind had stopped, and the raven swooping over our heads was only the usual size and winged away, ignoring us as if it had no interest in two such silly creatures.

I snorted. "Well, that was a lot of drama over nothing—" I broke off as I caught Alice's horrified look and, following her gaze, felt my stomach drop.

There, in the middle of the sunny meadow, was a large, flat gray rock. On the rock lay a dark-haired woman, her arm stretched out toward us and her claw-like fingers pointing at the scarf in Alice's hand.

"Hearne! You've finally come!" she collapsed as she said the words, her hand falling limply to graze the spring-green grass by the side of the rock.

It was like a scene from one of the plays put on by the Light

Faeries back home in Neverland, except instead of a puffed-up drama, the woman in front of us was covered in blood that flowed freely down the rock in scarlet trails before disappearing into the ground.

"This...this place doesn't feel like the Dreamworld," Alice said in a wavering voice, not quite looking at the woman in front of us though her head was turned in that direction.

"Doesn't it?" I asked faintly, trying not to be sick. Although I had been in many battles in Neverland, both on the side of the faeries and secretly on the side of the pirates, no one had ever been killed or even badly injured in one of them. The pixie magic was too strong and protective to allow that. My stomach churned at the sight of violence—and suffering—that was in front of us now.

"No, it doesn't. It has a completely different feel. I swear it's not part of the chessboard," Alice said a little more firmly. I watched as she chanced a look at the woman, and her face tinged green. "I suppose that's our Red Queen," she whimpered.

I glanced back at the woman. Her clothes were drenched with blood in varying stages of freshness, and her matted hair lay in straggled clumps around her head. But on her head was a crown of branches that matched the Red King's, the only difference being the huge thorns digging into her scalp. I watched as a droplet of blood welled up from one of the wounds and slid down the side of her temple onto the stone below.

I shuddered. The Red Queen's power was oppressive in this brilliant meadow. It pressed on us, in every blade of grass and every flower; the very stone she lay on seemed overburdened with power. I could barely stand to stay in the meadow, let alone look at her. She was giving her lifeblood and power away for some reason, and the pain and brilliance of it pricked at each nerve in my body. An expression of agony passed over the queen's face in her sleep, one exactly like what I had seen on my mother's face when she had extracted too much pixie dust over too long a time. I shuddered again.

Alice moved closer, clutching my hand hard enough to make

my bones ache. Her warmth as she pressed into my side was an anchor, one I could feel through my make-believe armor. "We have to help her," she said faintly. "We must. Even if the White Queen hadn't asked us to...."

"But how?" I whispered back, every fiber of my being rebelling at touching the living wound in front of us. *Surely anything we do will cause more pain, more wounds.*

"I—I suppose we could ask her if she wakes again," Alice said in a trembling voice, then moved closer. I followed in her wake, still not quite looking at the queen. Our feet squelched and stuck in the muddy ground as we came to the foot of the stone. I looked down, and all of the blood rushed from my face as I realized it wasn't muddy—at least not from rain. The ground was saturated with blood, and apparently, the grass was thriving in it.

"Oh no," Alice said faintly, tears dropping rapidly from her eyes and dripping to the ground as she bent toward the queen. I watched in detached horror as she reached up and wiped some blood from the queen's brow with the filthy rag. *She'll get an infection,* I thought idly, then almost laughed out loud. With each wound on her body open to whatever came her way, the last of the queen's worries would be an infection from a bit of dirt on a scarf.

Alice's gentle touch roused her, and the Red Queen opened her eyes, dark orbs filled with nightmares and horror as she muttered to herself something that sounded like "bread and butter, bread and butter."

"Hush now, it's alright," Alice soothed. "We've come to help, only we don't know how. Can we move you?"

"Can you?" she asked in a ghostly voice laced with hysteria. "Who are you? You look a little like my daughter, except I only ever had one, and you can't be her."

"Steady on," I said bracingly, recognizing the need for someone to take charge even though the other part of my brain rebelled at being involved in such a delicate situation. "She's not your daughter, so never mind all that. But she's—*we've*—come to help you. Are you well enough to move?"

The queen laughed—a burbling, horrible wet sound punctuated with a bubble that popped at the corner of her mouth. "Well enough? I dare say if I *could* move, I'd be well enough for anything. Or perhaps I'll never again be well enough for anything. It's difficult to tell these days. Too much living backward, you know," she said to Alice confidentially. "But it's the only way to get through the days. Interminably days, and it's never night here. How long has it never been night?"

"I'm sure I don't know," Alice said bracingly, picking up on my attempts to forestall a nervous breakdown—and not just by the queen. "I'm sure it's been much too long. If we move you, I'm sure we could find some nice cool shade, if not a bit of nighttime," she added soothingly.

"Perhaps under a tree?" the Red Queen asked hopefully.

"Yes, yes," I jumped in soothingly, "we could certainly manage a tree. We've been practically swimming in trees up until now."

"Let's get you up," said Alice. "That's the first thing." I moved forward, pushing all my reluctance at touching such a wounded creature aside and moving to the other side of the rock with horrible squelching footsteps.

"All together now, Peter and I will help. One, two, three." On three, I slipped my arm under the queen's shoulders as Alice supported her head, but the queen screamed piercingly, and I dropped her at once. Alice managed to lay her head back down gently, and I managed *not* to run as I scrubbed at the blood covering my arm bracers. *I'm glad I'm wearing armor right now, if only to keep the accursed blood off of me.*

"Can't we help you up?" Alice asked the queen with tears in her eyes. The queen lay there panting, her own eyes closed, and her mouth twisted in pain.

"I don't know, just let me think." She burbled another horribly wet laugh. "I've had all this time to think and to wish for help, and I've never thought about what could be done once it's arrived. My sister's spell holds me to this rock tightly, else I would have freed myself before now. So how does one break a spell from the Queen of Hearts?" she murmured to herself.

Alice and I stared at each other. Queen of Hearts? she mouthed, and I shook my head. I felt like every cell in my body was being rearranged in this sunny meadow. The horror of pain before me was like an out-of-body experience, but knowing that the Red Queen's sister did this to her made me want to climb out of my own skull. *Is it like this everywhere? One's family wringing out your very lifeblood for their betterment? And we give in because of love? Is that what makes the foundation of the world? Of every world? I thought breaking that tradition in Neverland would free us, but maybe rejoining the old country would simply bring us to another kind of bloodletting.*

"Is it like this where you're from?" I found myself asking Alice desperately. "Family spilling each other's blood—asking for a long, slow death to protect?"

Alice gave me a startled look. "No!" she said vehemently, shaking her head. "My family believes in duty, but not to that extent! We care for one another and help bear each other's burdens. To do something like this—" She gave me a startled look. "Is it like this where *you're* from?" she demanded.

I drew in a steadying breath. "Not for most. But for me, there will be a similar duty."

Alice reached across the queen and put her slight hand on my shoulder. "Then after we help the Red Queen, I will help you too. You won't bear that burden alone—or at all. I'm sure we can find a way together."

I couldn't help the smile that swept across my face, as unacceptable as it was in such a place of bloodshed and undying death. "I somehow believe you could help me, Alice." She gave me a wry smile but didn't answer, looking at the queen once more—who seemed to have passed out—and dropping her hand away from me again.

"First, we must find a way to help *her*," she said, gently passing the Red King's scarf under the queen's neck to wrap it around her shoulders like a shawl. Alice reached up to her own throat, unhooking an unassuming brooch from her waistcoat, and brought it down to use it to pin the makeshift shawl closed.

As she latched it shut, she drew her finger away with a sharp, "Ow!"

A drop of blood dripped off and splashed onto the Red Queen's cheek.

The instant it hit, power punched out from the queen, moving through us and out over the meadow. Alice and the queen both began screaming. I rushed around the stone to Alice's side.

"What is it?!" I begged her, but she could only scream, staring into my eyes with such haunting pain and agony, I couldn't stand it.

Desperate, I pushed magic toward the wound in her finger, but it resisted all my attempts, like oil trying to mix with water.

"How can I help?" I cried desperately, taking her in my arms and cradling her as we sat on the bloody ground beside the stone. Neither woman answered me, their screams echoing and confusing my thoughts.

"Come on, think," I told myself, rocking Alice and running my hand through her hair. "There must be a way to help, to end her pain—or at least share her burden like she would share mine."

Her words from earlier struck me. *Share the burden.* I knew a way to do that. It was why my mother had been pushing marriage on me—marriage to the most powerful being on our island. A pixie marriage bond helped share the burden of magic and pain—though the relief I gave her now might be negated if we couldn't end the lineage of pain in Neverland later.

"Alice, will you marry me?!" I asked her desperately, then laughed maniacally. "Of course, you shouldn't. I know you can't trust me—I deceived you when we first met and haven't done much to prove myself since then." Alice shook her head, and her distrust of me wounded me, but I didn't falter in my desire to help. "I know, I know this is absurd, but I'll always be true, and I'll always help you. And I can help you now, if you'll let me." She nodded furiously, still screaming, still locked on my eyes. I nodded once too. "I'll say the words and create a bond between us. If you accept it, just push your pain and magic and everything you can toward the bond, and it will lessen."

Without waiting for any sign from her, I used a blade to nip my finger. Pressing it to hers even as blood welled up, our blood mingled as I chanted the ancient vows.

"Now!" I screamed at her, and after a moment, I felt a surge of power between us. I pushed back, stuffing all the pixie magic and soothing and healing and *love* I felt in my heart toward her. Our magics clashed, and I felt the refreshing coolness of her adventurous spirit, and then everything went black.

CHAPTER THIRTEEN

Alice

The pain was too much. Pain is a silly word, some part of my brain that was still capable of thought mused. The pain I felt wasn't mine. It was the Red Queen's, but it was mine now. I had obviously created an accidental blood connection when I pricked my finger—an idiotic thing to do given the amount of magic steeped into the very air of this place—and the sheer volume of it was overwhelming, beyond overwhelming even.

"Alice, will you marry me?" Peter's voice echoed in my mind, in every fiber of my being. He was saying something, but in the pain, I couldn't hear very well, only see the green and gold of his heart magic pulsing and flaring bright, full of coolness and quiet and love. I wanted it. I wanted it badly. Somehow I knew it would quench the horror of the queen's pain, but even more, I knew it would soothe like a balm on my heart. He believed that I was more than a quiet mouse in a large family—not that I could be, but I was *already* more, and more beautiful than I could see myself. He was chastising himself now, saying he wasn't trustworthy, and I managed to shake my head in disagreement. I could focus slightly on him, and he asked again if I would let him help me. I nodded furiously.

His strange pixie magic washed over me, and in a flash, I

suddenly understood what spell he was weaving as his bloodied finger pressed to mine. *It's a marriage rite.* Much like the ancient Romany one I had studied years ago—and that I knew my sister had used to marry Petro in secret.

In what was probably the most understandably selfish moment of my life, I reached—no, dove for it. I knew Peter was offering it in a moment of distress, but I could feel, too, that he was sincere in it and that his fledgling love was there, and I wanted it badly—not just as a balm, but as my own and for myself.

As I reached out, I could feel him channeling a soothing healing spell toward me, and I opened my heart, welcoming his magic with as much love as I could muster, hoping the few little scraps I knew about love would be enough for a good foundation for us. I knew I would support him, grow with him, and let him support me back. I had so many loving couples as examples that I hoped to emulate, and from what I gathered, he had none. But together, we could forge our own path—as long as we started in this honest place.

His magic engulfed me, warm and bright, loud and joyful, and I closed my eyes, meeting it with a rising joy as I felt my heart unfold as I repeated the words I had heard him utter a moment ago. The heady surge of joy pushed back all pain, all agony, and the memory of suffering that had been my connection to the Red Queen and replaced it with Peter and me together. The moment seemed to stretch into an eternity filled with pulsing light and swirling eddies of a dancing breeze that I realized with contented surprise were the flavor of my spirit and magic—that spirit of adventure, as Peter had named it. *So it was there all along.*

Much too soon, the endless joy of that moment began to fade, and the present came rushing back in. I became aware just in time that Peter was fainting. I caught him against me before he could bash his head against the stone altar, cradling his head and shifting until I could bear the weight of his body without too much strain.

"Peter?" I asked hesitantly, examining him closely. His chest was rising and falling, and his color was normal. After a second, his eyes fluttered open, and he smiled that mischievous smile at me. I felt the corner of my mouth crook up in response, then fall again as his expression folded.

"You're feeling better, obviously, but now you're stuck with me," he said with unusual seriousness.

"Oh, I'm quite happy to be stuck with you," I responded honestly, "but I know *you* won't like feeling trapped with me. Is there nothing to be done? I'd hate for you to feel like you had to trail around after me for the rest of our lives. How long do faeries live, incidentally?"

"A couple hundred years, usually," he answered offhand. "But I'm only twenty-five, so it will be a long time to be stuck together."

"Well, humans usually only live to be a hundred, at the most," I replied, realizing my arms were still partially around him but not caring to draw back. "So you'll be rid of me before too long, I expect. Although I'm only twenty-one—nearly twenty-one, that is—so it will be a long time until then."

"Your life will lengthen to match his," the Red Queen's rusty voice cut in, and the two of us turned in our seats on the squishy ground to face her, Peter's arm snaking around my waist to draw me closer to him almost unconsciously. The gesture thrilled me, even though I knew his interest and protectiveness wouldn't last long. It wasn't in his nature, I expected, and I would never hobble someone from being themselves to soothe my insecurities. But I could enjoy his attention while it lasted.

"You can move!" Peter exclaimed, and I realized the Red Queen had managed to sit up, and was even now swinging her legs around to the side of the stone table. I jumped up to help her, but she waved me off.

"Yes, I can move now. It seems that some combination of the blood connection Alice accidentally worked when she pricked her finger and the marriage bond you two cemented—or the unique combination of magic that we all three have, or the time of day, or something else that we none of us know—was enough to break the spells my sister wrought on me all those years ago." The queen gingerly put each foot on the ground but took a minute to draw in a deep breath as she wiped at the blood on her brow.

"Here," Peter said, stepping forward and offering a snow-white silk handkerchief to the queen. As she took it, he turned back to me and produced another. "Let me see your finger," he said gently, taking my proffered hand and murmuring a healing spell before tying the handkerchief gently but firmly in place.

I watched him in amusement. "Don't you trust me to heal my own wounds?"

His eyes flicked to mine with a half smile. "I'd rather heal them myself."

My smile softened, and I leaned forward to kiss his cheek. "Why the handkerchief?" I asked after I pulled away, holding up my awkwardly bandaged hand.

He shrugged. "I've seen the humans do so on Neverland when they're hurt and don't want to use magic to heal. And even when they do accept a healing spell, the pixie magic sometimes takes a while to settle. They usually stem the bleeding with a compress in the meantime. I didn't know how you would take to the pixie magic, and I didn't want to chance it."

My heart warmed further at his caring attention. "I think the pixie magic likes me," I told him, unwrapping the bandage and showing him the wound I had already felt healing. The skin on my finger was whole and unblemished. "But this, I'll keep," I declared saucily, waving the handkerchief once before stuffing it in my waistcoat pocket.

"Well, mine doesn't seem to be doing its job," the Red Queen interjected, and we glanced up to see her holding out a completely soaked handkerchief. A moment later, it was gone, incinerated with a brief flash of magic. The queen grinned sharply. "I didn't want to leave an object with my blood on it lying around. My apologies, Master Peter."

She stretched her arms out, her grin widening even as more

wounds were revealed. "I can't tell you how good that felt. I haven't used magic in over a thousand years. Can you imagine how uncomfortable it's been to have it buzzing under my skin all that time? Ever leaching out through the blood spell, never reaching its true potential?"

Not knowing what to say to such a horrible thing, I stood up, Peter following a moment later. "I imagine we should leave this place quickly," I told the queen. "If your sister notices we've interrupted her spell, we don't want to be here when she shows up. Besides, your other sister is searching for you, too. Perhaps we can summon her if we find a way out of the meadow. Um, Your Majesty," I added belatedly, dipping a short curtsy.

The queen smiled. "Call me Aife, child. After all, if what I feel from your magic is correct, you are my many times great-granddaughter." Her smile faltered even as my jaw dropped. She added in a low tone, "I always knew I would outlive my daughter in this world, but I never imagined it would be like this—that I wouldn't be there to shepherd her through to the next life when she went," her voice broke, and she shook her head. "The time for that grief is long past and has not yet come again. You spoke wisely, Alice. Let us depart from this accursed place."

CHAPTER FOURTEEN

Peter

The Red Queen staggered as she took her first few steps—which is to be expected if she had been chained to that rock by magic for a millennium. Alice and I propped her up as best we could, and I did my best to ignore the blood smearing across my white armor.

We stumbled across the grass together, our footsteps squelching and splashing wetly on the boggy ground, splattering crimson mud with every lurch forward. Alice looked quite pale, but the Red Queen seemed to gain a little strength the further we got from the stone table.

After a time, we encountered an ancient-looking wooden boat tied to a post at an unremarkable spot on the marshy ground. I say unremarkable because there was no dock nor a path to the boat—nor was the post set into a particularly dry patch of ground. It seemed to appear there, weatherbeaten, bloodstained, and inexplicably moored securely.

"Let's get in," Alice urged. I shifted the queen's weight toward her, then hopped into the small watercraft, turning to help first the queen, then Alice, into the boat. Once they were settled, I attempted to squeeze onto the bench next to Alice and almost upset the entire craft. The queen went very white under all the blood, so I stepped into the air to allow the boat to resume its equilibrium.

"Perhaps I should fly instead of upsetting the boat again," I said dubiously, then crooked a grin at Alice's obvious delight in seeing me fly. I couldn't help turning a flip, then hovered in the air, my hands on my hips. "If I had more pixie dust, I'd fly us all across," I told her cheekily.

"When I get to Neverland, I would love to fly," she said breathlessly.

I winked at her. "Then fly you shall."

"As much as I remember how intoxicating young love was," the Red Queen interrupted, "it is less so for those of us on the outside. As grateful as I am for your assistance in freeing me, we are none of us free yet. And I fear this lake holds horrors in its depths."

"Let's go, then," said Alice reassuringly, then took up the oars with more experience and vigor than I had thought she'd have. *I guess her royal upbringing included rowing at some point?* She was a continuous well of surprise. I smiled at my new wife with contentment that surprised me.

As soon as I was sure Alice had the hang of the oars and that there weren't any creatures waiting to pounce on the two occupants of the boat, I soared as high into the sky as I dared, hoping the spells on my armor would shield me from prying eyes. I couldn't see very far, but I *just* thought I could see the other end of the row—or a shoreline, at any rate—and flew back down to tell Alice. I found her chattering away with the Red Queen, which was highly amusing since she was treating the blood-soaked ancient magical being who helped create the foundations of our world as if she were a long-lost aunt she hadn't seen in a long time. *I suppose she is a long-lost family member if what the queen said was right.* I felt a thrum of amusement that wasn't mine somewhere in the back of my heart and grinned as I soared back into the air again. My heart seemed lighter than I had ever known since I had exchanged vows with Alice. It was as though all the windows of that organ had been opened up and fresh air allowed in to blow away the cobwebs. Whatever came next would be better because of Alice, and whatever I needed to face or fix would be possible because of her.

After what felt like hours but was probably no more than thirty minutes, the boat ran aground. After a brief consultation, it was decided that I would fly Alice over, and come back for the queen.

The flight with Alice was too brief. The feeling of her securely in my arms made me never want to let go, and at the same time, it made me believe I could be a White Knight in truth—that I would fight any battle for her love, win any tournament for her favor, bear any hard thing for her betterment. As we touched down on the dim shoreline, she pulled her arms tighter around my neck and gave me a brief kiss, her lips soft and thin. The touch stunned me and was all too brief. When she pulled back, I dipped my head to press my forehead to hers, not having the words to tell everything in my heart.

"I wish I could take you home to Neverland—or better yet, find our way into your world. I would whisk you away to some lonely place and have you all to myself," I said finally as she began to pull away. A blush spread across her nose, but her smile was full of confidence.

"I shall hold you to that," she whispered. "But to get there, we'll have to finish helping the Red Queen. I can't shake the feeling that messing this up will bring doom upon us all." She shivered and let me pull her into the warmth of my embrace for one more minute, then pushed me gently away. "Go get the queen. I'll wait here, don't worry."

My body rebelled at the idea of letting her go. She was mine. Mine to look after and love. And I didn't want to leave my new wife anywhere, let alone on this forsaken shore. *I haven't even kissed her yet.*

"I just realized," I said quietly, looking into her eyes. "We've been married for—well, I should think maybe a whole hour—and I've never even kissed you."

Alice's face went red, and a shy smile twisted her lips. She hesitated for a moment, then whispered, "Better make it quick then."

I dipped my head down, pausing to take a breath filled with vanilla and orange and Alice, then pressed my lips to hers.

The world stopped moving.

Too late, I realized that this was a trap—a honeyed trap that I would happily die in. There was no mystifying Dreamland, no Neverland problem, only Alice and the promise of tomorrow as she kissed me.

I pulled back, some reflex reminding me that I had a job to do, but I found that I couldn't. Instead, I peppered her with more soft, sweet kisses, pressing them against her lips, her cheeks, her eyes and nose. After a moment, she sighed and framed my face with her hands, anchoring me to her and giving me one last, slow kiss before pushing me away again.

We stared at each other for a moment, her dazed eyes surely reflecting my own.

"Go now," she said wistfully, "and come back quickly." I huffed a disappointed breath, then pressed one more fierce kiss to her mouth and stepped back, reluctantly flying off.

A few dazed minutes of flying later, I realized I should have already found the run-aground boat with the bloodied Red Queen. Sweeping my head back and forth with increasing urgency, I caught a glimpse of something in the distance and realized it had somehow gone adrift. It had already carried the queen far down the coastline.

I hovered in the air, looking back toward Alice, who sat calmly where I had left her, and debated flying back to tell her what had happened. *It would take too long—I would probably lose the queen. I tore* my gaze away and darted toward Aife.

CHAPTER FIFTEEN

Alice

Waves rippled gently along the marshy shoreline. I tried not to look at them, as a millennium of the Red Queen's blood had mixed with the water of the border stream so thoroughly that I fancied it was more blood than water. I shivered to think of what the power in her blood was being used for, and I didn't like the little whispers of magic that brushed at my ears when I did look a little too long. Rust-colored sparkles hovered over the water here and there, where magic was being pulled from the viscous flow. It must be the Queen of Hearts siphoning her sister's power. She used Aife's blood for evil magic, to create suffering and horrors. The stench of the rancid water and the horror of the foul magic was overwhelming, and I looked anxiously into the distance to where our boat had run aground.

I couldn't see it. I couldn't see Peter, either. I strained my eyes, but there was nothing. Suddenly I felt the weight of my solitude as if it were a blanket smothering me. I hadn't been alone since I met Peter in that shadow parlor in the mirror palace of my home. His presence had been a ray of tricksy sunshine ever since that moment, and now—now I was married to that ray of sunshine, with a future of butterfly-stirring kisses ahead of me. I smiled and pressed my hands to my cheeks at the memories of his lips on mine. I closed my eyes, taking a deep breath to steady my swirling emotions—which worked wonderfully well since the stench of the marsh came with it. I was snapped back to my current reality, seated at the side of evil in a land that, while it must have been intended for better, had turned into a refuge of monsters and nightmares.

I took a few steps toward the marshy edge of the river but drew back when my foot sunk into the watery sludge. Scanning the dreary horizon, which faded into steely gloom before I could see the other edge of the river, I searched desperately for a glimpse of either Peter in flight or the Red Queen in the little boat. I saw neither.

Wrapping my arms around my waist, I hugged myself close. *Surely they'll be back soon. Perhaps I'm looking in the wrong direction. Or probably, I can't see that far away. The river is broad, and Peter did fly with me for several minutes before we crossed the marsh.*

I shivered again, missing Peter's lighthearted—if mercurial—warmth. I tried several times to reach out with my newfound affinity with the Dreamworld, but as soon as I did, I drew back—a sensation like hot coals striking my nerves that I somehow knew was from the nearby river. I wasn't adept enough yet to block such a thing out.

A familiar coolness settled over my heart as the minutes ticked by, and I realized Peter and the queen might not be coming back any time soon. This was nothing new, being left behind as the more important people fulfilled their duty. My role was always to support, and I loved being able to do that for my loved ones. But for a few moments when we said our vows—and when he gave me those intoxicating kisses!—I felt I was Peter's priority. And the charge from the White Queen to save her sister felt almost as if I had a purpose of my own—a real calling that needed my odd talents. *Perhaps it was a bit naive of me to assume I would be important in this quest. It's one of Queens and Nightmares, after all.*

As there was no sun to mark the progress of time, I began

counting. After reaching one thousand, the creeping sense of doom that could be from the proximity of foul magic or *could be my connection to the Dreamworld warning me that time was short* became too much.

Maybe Peter decided to fly her to the last row after all. It would make sense to get her safely to the end. And maybe he couldn't come back to tell me of the change of plans. It made sense. And despite Peter's protestations that I needed a guide through the Dreamworld, only a couple of rows were left. Surely I could do this on my own. Reality settled over me like honey dripping slowly from the comb, sinking thickly into my bones. I was back to myself, the little butterfly floating from task to task, tracing my way through life. It was a relief, almost, to realize I just had to look after myself, that I wasn't the heroine in this story, and that the world's fate didn't rest on my actions. I simply had an appointment to keep and help to offer if it was wanted.

"Right then, better get moving." I turned, stopped a moment to consider, then looked around to see if there was anything I could use to leave a message. The only things in abundance were dead and dying reeds and cattails, so I gathered an armful of those, arranged them in the shape of an arrow on the ground, pointing the way I was going, then shrugged and walked on. There wasn't much else I could do, and the sense that I should be moving was getting stronger and stronger. So I moved.

The gray gloom hovering around my periphery reminded me of the fog that sometimes descended in Dryfaeston. I could almost be walking in the nature preserve at night if I had gone off the path near the river. And if all the buzzing life in the nature preserve had fallen silent. And the noises of the city were stopped. And the streetlights had gone out. I shivered. There was only so far that imagination could take you.

But maybe it can take you further than you think. I stopped suddenly as I came upon a gray stone wall, sturdy, well-laid, and stretching into the distance on either side of me. It was the same color as the gloom around me, so it was no wonder I hadn't seen it—if I hadn't conjured it myself, wishing for the city walls of

Dryfaeston and the night watch that would be stationed there.

Just as the night watch popped into my mind, a voice called down to me from the top of the wall.

"Tell me your name and your business," it demanded in a papery, but forceful tone.

"Alice," I said dutifully, remembering belatedly that Peter had cautioned me against giving my name. "And I'm simply trying to get through this row safely."

"This is my row," the voice answered, "or at least it belongs to my master, and I am looking after it for him until he returns. What does Alice mean?"

I blinked up, trying to make out the owner of the voice. He seemed to be sitting on the top of the wall, his spindly legs hanging down and his large, oval face peering at me with a peevish expression. "Why does it matter what my name means?" I asked curiously, wondering at the same time why he was sitting on the wall instead of merely looking over it, "And aren't you afraid of falling off that wall?"

"Not at all," he replied, answering my second question first. "I've been sitting on this wall longer than *you've* been alive, I wager," he continued triumphantly. "You're human, aren't you?"

"Aren't you?" I asked back and immediately regretted it when he flinched backward, almost unseating himself.

"Human?! Me?" he demanded. "What drivel! How in the world did you get that impression? I may be elderly, but I'm not so old that my magic has completely deserted me. Haven't you ever seen a fae before?"

"No, I haven't!" I exclaimed delightedly, then gasped as he rocked backward yet again. "Do please come down from that wall," I pleaded. "It doesn't seem entirely safe."

The fae looked down his nose at me with a superior attitude. "Why should it be entirely safe? Nothing is *entirely* safe, especially not in this plane of existence. What an odd child you seem to be."

"I'm not a child," I protested, wincing a little at the necessary childishness of that statement. "I'm almost twenty-one."

"*Almost* twenty-one, is it? Which means twenty, of course. A very awkward age for humans, if I remember correctly. Almost infantile for a fae, but if I learned my races correctly, it's the age of maturity for a human. All the freedom of an adult, but the experience of a child. Very awkward, indeed," he said firmly. "Does your mother know you've wandered in here?"

"Well, no," I admitted, then remembered I probably shouldn't be giving such information to a stranger. "But I'm here with friends, so *they* know. Does your master know you're sitting on walls and interrogating strangers?"

"Of course he does. After all, he sees everything," he said scornfully, pointing upward as if that was supposed to mean anything to me. "Wouldn't be a good King of the Heavens if he didn't." He dropped his hand to scratch at the sparse gray hair on his head. "Though he'd be a better one if he could find his queen—or his mind for that matter," he added as if to himself. I didn't know what to say, so I cast around for a different subject. My eyes lit upon the cravat he was wearing, which was so colorful as to be visible even from the height he was sitting at.

"What a wonderful cravat!" I exclaimed, then frowned. "Or is it a collar?" I asked doubtfully.

"It's a *sigil*," he replied severely, stroking the cloth with his hand, which made the design glow faintly. "I was given it by the White King himself when I was appointed his steward. It was born by the steward before me, and the one before him, and so on." His gaze drifted upward. "Of late, I have wondered if I am to be the last to bear it." His eyes flashed down to me. "Surely he hasn't sent *you* to take up the mantle."

I drew in a deep breath. "No, no indeed. I was sent by the White Queen—" the fae interrupted me with a great shout and clapped his hands.

"Why didn't you say so at once, child? Has she been found? She must be looking for her king. Come up! You must come up at once and give me your news!"

With that, he jumped down from sight, and I stared at the space he had lately occupied in stupefaction. *Surely he doesn't think I can fly up there?*

    A moment later, the notion was swept from my head as a door appeared in the wall in front of me. It swung open and the fae appeared on the other side, ushering me through with a quick glance around before slamming the door shut and wiping its existence from the face of the wall again. I swallowed nervously, wondering if I had made the right choice by coming inside. There was no way out.

CHAPTER SIXTEEN

Peter

As I flew down the river, my heart got heavier and heavier, like a rock in my chest. I bobbed lower to get a better look at something dark on the water, now higher to get a better view of the whole river, hoping I would find the Red Queen quickly and reunite with Alice before she became worried.

The minutes stretched on, and I worried that I had missed the queen and the little boat in my haste through the gloom, so I slowed my flight, taking more time to fly over each section of the river and forcing myself to focus on the search instead of the growing distance between me and my heart. A raven swooped from overhead, turning and banking some way up the river, then flapping toward the forest, I watched it's flight for a moment, then turned my gaze back to the water.

Finally, I spotted the little boat—with its pale passenger lying in it, still marked with blood—just as it came upon some rapids in the river.

"Not if I can help it!" I growled to no one as I dove, arrowing toward the boat with all the speed I could muster. In a flash, I was touching down into the vessel, trying not to rock the boat any more than it already was. The queen's eyes fluttered open at my presence, and she smiled to see me.

"Your timing could be improved," she said with a bloody cough. I frowned my offended pride at her but didn't bother to argue. *I just need to grab her and get to Alice.*

Water sloshed over the side of the boat as it rocked perilously, and I grimaced at the red sheen it left on my skin even as I bent forward to lift the queen into my arms. She was surprisingly light. She looked as muscular and strong as you'd expect a Shepherd of the Wilderness to appear, but she was lighter even than Alice had been. A shudder wracked my spine as I realized it was probably the result of unknown tortures over the years at her sister's hand.

Another wave of red sloshed over the side of the boat, and I sprang into the air to avoid it, shifting the queen into a more secure position. She seemed to have lost consciousness again and couldn't help by holding herself up like Alice had, so flying was quite a bit trickier with her than it had been with my wife.

My wife. My heart squeezed at the thought of her alone on the shore of this accursed river.

I turned and flew back the way I had come. Following my trail was easy—I had followed the river to begin with and now just needed to retrace its course. Unfortunately, the flight was increasingly more difficult. The added burden of another person, and one whose bleeding wounds and inability to stay conscious for more than a few minutes, made her impossible to keep hold of. More of my effort went into keeping her aloft than in speeding through the air.

After a while, I watched the shoreline more carefully, hoping to see Alice waiting patiently to be reunited with us. My heart pumped harder with every moment that passed and I didn't see her. I circled a section of shoreline that I thought was near the place I had left her, but she wasn't there. *I'm sure this is the place.* I swept down to look more closely.

A dark shape came into view as I flew closer, but before I could land, I realized it wasn't Alice at all. It was a massive monster with scaly skin, short stubby legs, and a huge narrow head that ended in sharp, toothy jaws that crunched on something.

For a moment, my heart stopped, wondering if it had attacked Alice in my absence. Then it started again, and I realized it was chewing on cattails. "I thought crocodiles ate meat," I muttered, for certainly it was a crocodile, or a crocodile-like creature, of which I was familiar enough from the swamp in Neverland.

I shifted the queen in my arms and risked a blast of magic, successfully frightening away the crocodile and waking the queen up. I settled onto the ground and helped her sit, then went to look at the pile of cattails that had so interested the crocodile.

Though they were a broken mess now, it was apparent they had been gathered together by design. *It would be just like Alice to provide a meal for a crocodile she met here without regard for her safety.* I was confident the crocodile hadn't gotten Alice—I realized that would have known from our bonding spell—but I still didn't know where she had gone. I slowly looked around the landscape and saw nothing but gloomy trees and scrub brush.

"Alice must have moved on," I said to Aife when I turned back to her and realized she was still awake. "I don't know where she's gone, but I know from our bonding spell that she's okay."

The queen coughed again and nodded. "That same bond can be used to find her, but we will need somewhere safe for me to teach you."

"This is the Steward's row, isn't it?" I asked the queen, who merely shrugged. "I'm almost certain it is. I have a bolthole here that should be safe enough to hide in while we locate Alice."

Aife nodded doggedly and allowed me to put an arm under her shoulders to help her limp forward. I had used much of my pixie dust flying to find her, and as much as I wished we could simply fly to the bolthole, I didn't want to attract attention if I could avoid it, and I wanted to save my pixie dust in case we encountered an emergency—not to mention needing it to get back to Neverland.

We slowed to a crawl as we approached the hideout, the queen managing on her own and laying down for rests each time I stopped to survey our surroundings. Other than a few detached shadows that slinked here and there through the trees, we didn't run into anything too ominous. It was a welcome surprise, as this section of the Dreamworld fairly crawled with Nightmares usually. The Steward claimed dominion over this row, but as he never came out of his tower, chaos was the true ruler.

Not trusting our luck to last, I helped Aife crowd into the hollowed-out tree trunk that served as the main entrance to the hideout and traced the spell that would take us down. A rush of air was our only warning before the floor dropped out beneath us, and we were deposited on the usual stack of moss, dead leaves, and scavenged blankets and cushions.

The air seemed to rush out of Aife's lungs, and I winced as I remembered the abuse her body had recently been released from. Dropping ten feet—even onto a soft surface—probably wasn't helping the healing process.

Before I could ask if she needed help, I heard a footstep followed by the cold sting of a knife point held to my neck. My eyes flicked up to find a dark-haired man with a thunderous expression looming over me. *We've been discovered.*

CHAPTER SEVENTEEN

Alice

"Follow me," the fae intoned from on high, this time because of his immense stature, not because he was sitting on a wall. I had thought his voice sounded papery when I first heard him, and now I realized his skin was also rather papery, and he moved as if he were made of paper—with floating steps and a crinkly sort of rustle.

He turned away, his head bobbing as he strode toward a tower in the middle of the courtyard, and I found myself following him without fear. He seemed to be a dour person and a vexing conversationalist, but he didn't feel wicked—not in the way the river did. *Besides, a steward of the White King couldn't be wicked, could he?*

Still, he wasn't how I had pictured a fae would be. In the books I had seen they were sharp and glittering. This steward seemed more inclined to be stuffy and pedantic.

"Come, come!" he called over his shoulder, and I scurried to keep up. Before long, we had entered the tower and climbed a set of winding stone stairs covered by a deep blue carpet, with wall hangings fluttering as we went by. Glowing lights lit our way dimly, not strong enough to illuminate the shadowy recesses here and there, but enough to prevent a fall.

At last, we came to the top of the tower and my feet slowed to a stop, even as the Steward began fiddling with things on a table further in. The top of the tower was one immense room, with what I recognized as a telescope similar to the ones used by mages dedicated to the White King in Dryfaeston. Everywhere were stacks of books and charts with lists, magical objects fairly pulsing under the strength of their spells, and a general shabby untidiness that seemed to mark every scholar who followed this particular Kingly Shepherd.

"I thought I detected a hint of the White Queen's magic about you, and now that you're in the room with me, I can hear it loud and clear," the fae chattered at me as he moved around the room. "But what's more, I can feel—ah yes, here it is," he exclaimed in satisfaction as he pulled an enormous tome off the shelf before breaking into a wracking cough when he flipped it open, scattering a cloud of dust everywhere. I moved forward, pounded him on the back to help clear the cough, then drew back as he shrieked.

"I'm sorry!" I exclaimed. "I was only trying to help!"

"Help?! By breaking my back?" he howled petulantly. I looked at his back dubiously, then recoiled as I saw little cracks snaking up from beneath the neckline of his old-fashioned, courtly robes.

"Is your back really breaking?" I asked anxiously, gesturing to the lines. "What can I do to fix it?"

"Fix it?!" he wheezed dubiously, then laughed hoarsely and coughed once more before regaining his voice. "There's no fixing it, Your Highness. It comes with living so long in the Land of Dreams without walking in the natural world."

"Then perhaps I could help you find your way back—"

The steward laughed. "Back? Back?!" he demanded. "I wouldn't go back for all the knowledge in the heavens. That *queen*," he spit venomously, "she ruined my lands a thousand years ago. There is nothing for me to go back to, and if anything has grown in its place since then, I wouldn't connect with it for anything—twisted darkness is all it would hold. At least until the Kings and Queens come again," he added, then shook his head and gave me a kindly smile, "There is no going home for me, child. Only holding the tower and living long enough to pass the stewardship on, if I may. But it was kind of you to think of me. And I suppose if you've never met a fae before, you wouldn't know what happens to us when we can't walk among our own lands." He turned back to his book and heaved a heavy sigh. "And since you've never met one, I suppose that means no fae has returned to our lands in all this time. I wonder—" He shook his head and began flipping through pages.

"Ah. Here we are," he said triumphantly, pointing to a line and beckoning me closer.

I looked at the page curiously, then with equal parts wonder and suspicion. "That's my name!" I exclaimed. "Why did you pretend not to know me?"

"I don't know you from Guinevere!" he replied in an offended tone. "You can't expect me to be tracking the descendants of the Red Queen when I serve the White King."

"But you have a book with my name in it! Who put my name there if not you?"

"Why would *I* add names to the Red Book of Lineage? The book keeps itself, obviously. We only have a copy on the shelf because the Red Queen is the White King's sister-in-law, and he gifted some of his magic to her daughter's subjects. The king may only speak in riddles these days, but the dance of stars has enough power yet for the book to know what to record."

I frowned at his words, only understanding half of them, and looked back down at my name, written prettily in red ink at the bottom of a page. Next to it were all my siblings—and Briar, I was delighted to see, marked with a marriage line to Raleigh —, parents, grandparents, and nieces. As I looked, I watched in wonder as another name appeared, as if an invisible hand was writing it before my eyes. A pair of golden lines appeared under my name, and below them was written Peter Pan, Prince of Neverland, and a date. I gasped. The book was recording my marriage! And the date was only a few days after I had entered the Dreamworld.

"So I've been here for days," I murmured under my breath.

"You've been lately married?" the steward asked curiously, looking at me under bushy eyebrows. "Is that the *friend* you mentioned earlier? Where is he?"

"I—well, yes, it was. He's off helping the Red Queen—" I stopped and looked at him wide-eyed, wondering if I should tell him anything more.

"So you've found your foremother!" the steward exclaimed. "That's what the unexpected alignment in the stars that has been coming on means!" He frowned. "But she's not here with you now. Your husband is helping, you say?"

"Yes—I think so anyway. I was waiting for them on the shore before I saw you, but they never came. We're trying to get to the last row, but she's not doing well, and I think he decided to fly her there. That's why I'm trying to get through *your* row. I'm trying to meet them at the last row. The White Queen asked me to," I explained earnestly, hoping against hope that this odd fae could help me.

"The White Queen," he repeated with a rapturous expression. "Where did you find her? Is she coming here?"

I shook my head. "I don't know. I only met her by chance, and she seems to be under some sort of curse. She's not all *there*, if that makes sense. Only part of her is there, sometimes."

The fae sunk into himself, the feverish joy from a moment ago leaking out. "It was too much to hope for. Still, the alignment in the stars is there. The White King must see something in the heavenly dance and is arranging it as he can. Come, let us look."

He motioned me forward, and I followed him up onto the platform of the telescope. As he began adjusting the dials, the raftered ceiling of the tower melted away, turning translucent, or perhaps simply ceasing to exist, as a blazing starry sky revealed itself.

"How beautiful!" I exclaimed, but the fae ignored me. After a few moments, he seemed to have the telescope focused on something and began jotting down notes and entering things into a chart on the tables on each side of the telescope, muttering to himself all the time. Finally, he stepped back and looked at me.

"There, what do you think of that?!" he asked, pointing to the viewing aperture.

I stepped forward and, peering into the aperture, took in a series of stars and planets which I recognized from my time with the telescope at home—though never in such clarity.

"The Hunter and Huntress are in opposition," I began, "as they often are this time of year—" the fae interrupted me with a snort.

"As they often are? You, young pup, know nothing of the stars. It's only these last few hundreds of years that they've been in opposition. In fact—yes, that *must* be what the king is trying to tell me. Come along." The fae whisked me off the platform, and I tried not to knock over piles of papers as we weaved across the tower to a bookshelf next to the opposite wall.

"Have you seen *this* before?" he asked triumphantly, pulling a book from the shelf. The title was worked in gold on the deep red cover. *The Jabberwocky*.

"Yes, actually, almost as soon as I entered the Dreamworld—"

"Hah! I knew it wasn't a coincidence. Blood calls to blood, they say. Now, I assume you don't know what it says, as humans have a devastating lack of understanding when it comes to languages."

"Well, no," I answered, feeling a little offended on my own behalf and that of my race. "I know several different languages, but—"

"Several!" the fae exclaimed, "several, she says as if knowing a handful of human languages out of all the languages of men and elves, fae and faerie, celestial and terrestrial, is some sort of accomplishment."

I stared at him in wonder. "How many do *you* know?" I asked in delight.

"Oh, well," he said bashfully, two spots of color appearing on his papery skin as he fiddled with his sigil. "Only a handful of each, truth be told. It's been a millennium since I've had to use any. Even a fae is bound to get rusty without practice."

I raised my eyebrow. *He was quick to make me feel small, but I don't think he knows as many as he'd like to admit.*

"Still," he hurried on, "I know this one well enough. Let me tell you the gist of the tale as I begin to think you may not have time to linger and read it through. It tells the story of the Red King's search for his true love, and the agony of his heart as he abandoned his daughter to rule her country in the natural world so he could find his queen in this one. But over the long years, the heartache he endured in the search, and the evil he has fought that carries the taint of his wife's magic, he has turned to his Beastly nature to endure. Now he is to be found in his dragon form more often than not, and if something is not done soon, it is feared that he will never leave it again."

"So if we reunite them, he will be saved and their love restored?" I asked.

"No!" the steward shouted, pressing a hand to his temple. "I'm remembering now how *simply* humans see everything. Didn't you hear me say the evil here is brushed with the Red Queen's tainted magic? He hunts her now not to be reunited, but to end her magic."

"But it's not her fault! Her sister is the one who captured her —"

"That I know, child, and the Red King may know it still, somewhere deep inside. But the Red Queen's magic is what has twisted everything here, and in other realms as well, I wager. To the Red King's tortured mind, he may only be able to think of ending the suffering—his own, the world's, and his some-time queen's."

I drew back in horror, and the fae's eyes softened. "Not a nice thing to think of your forefather, I imagine. But this world is not a *nice* place. Not now."

"Here," he grumbled, noting my look of despair. "I suppose I'm still strong enough to gift you with a language for my troubles," he said apologetically, pushing the book into my hands and pressing his palm to my forehead. I frowned at his touch, my forehead wrinkling under his cold palm, but I stood patiently. After a moment, I felt a whispery spell enter my forehead. With a gasp, I stepped back when the magic stopped, filled with wonder as new words and ideas filled my mind.

The steward stumbled backward as well, tumbling into a nearby chair and rubbing his forehead. "That took more energy than I remembered. What fun getting older has turned out to be," he muttered sardonically.

"This is—it's incredible!" I exclaimed, barely able to form words around the new ones rushing through my mind. "Thank you!"

"You're welcome, child, but I can do nothing more. I must rest, and you must go. If you take the red door on the wall and walk straight on from it, you will find the fastest way through the rest of the square. I regret I cannot take you there myself.

I dipped a curtsy. "Thank you for your help—I'm sorry, I don't think I ever asked your name!" I exclaimed.

The old fae smiled widely, his grin somehow ugly and endearing at the same time. "Steward Humphrey, at your service, Princess Alice."

"I shall mention you to the White Queen if I see her again," I promised, and the fae's eyes filled with tears.

"Then I will be grateful to you. If she were to come here, perhaps her power would be enough to draw the White King down from the heavens again. Now go. There is no time to waste while the planets are thus aligned. And the part you are to play..." he trailed off, shaking his head. "Simply walk the path in front of you, child, and take the book with you!"

I nodded, clutching the Jabberwocky book to my chest, then backed away as he closed his eyes and seemingly settled back into his chair for a nap. Turning, I fled the tower and took the red door out of the courtyard.

CHAPTER EIGHTEEN

Peter

Allowing an expression of fear to cross my face instead of the surge of rage I truly felt in finding a stranger in my safehouse, I opened my mouth as if to plead for mercy. Instead, I used the millisecond the stranger relaxed as he anticipated my words to spring backward into the air and out of reach, hovering over Aife.

"Watch out—" a familiar voice called, then chuckled. "I meant to warn you he can fly."

"Wendy?" I asked disbelievingly as she stepped out of one of the shadowy recesses of our hideout. "Do you know this man?"

"Not really," she said nonchalantly, stepping forward again until she was even with him.

The man kept his blade drawn and his eyes on me even as he asked her, "Are these people enemies?"

"No—well, I don't know the waif he's picked up, so she might be—but this is my friend, Peter," she replied, crossing her arms over her chest and scowling at Aife.

"Ah," the man said perfunctorily and stood a little straighter—though I noticed he didn't sheath his knife. He seemed almost relaxed at first glance, but a loose-limbed readiness to how he carried himself reminded me of the more serious-minded pirates on Neverland. I instantly disliked him. I dislike anyone who is serious-minded.

Except Alice, I amended quickly. *Although she's not so much serious-minded as she is simply comfortable with herself, and so lacking in ego that she never minds the situation she's found herself in. There's a difference.*

"Who is *he*?" I asked accusingly. "You promised never to bring strangers here, yet you say you don't know him!"

"*You've* brought a stranger," Wendy shot back accusingly, tipping her head toward Aife, who was breathing shallowly on the floor with her eyes still shut.

"She's not exactly a stranger," I replied, lowering to the floor to stand beside the Shepherd. "Besides, this is my safe house, so if I want to change the rules, I can."

"Oh, I like that," Wendy said, rolling her eyes. "Just like you to change the rules to suit yourself on a moment's notice. Well, Hook here isn't *exactly* a stranger, either. He's been following me around for ages and has mostly avoided being a nuisance. It's his first time in the Dreamworld, and as I was the first thing he saw upon entering, he thinks I'm the one who will lead him to the end of his quest. He's sort of imprinted on me, you know, like an orphaned wolf cub or something."

I raised my eyebrows and glanced at Wendy's "wolf cub," who stood a few inches taller than me and looked handy with a blade.

"Look, just trust me, he's fine. Who's that?" she asked again, looking at the battered Aife with mingled disgust and concern. "She's seen better days, whoever she is. Why haven't you healed her? That's just like you to save someone from a Nightmare attack only to let them bleed out from their wounds on the way back."

She started to move toward Aife as if to help her, but I motioned her back. "There's no point. We already tried to heal her wounds, but they were made by something—or someone— much stronger than us. She's been fine so far. I think the drop from the entrance knocked her out. Just…just help me get her to one of the beds over there, and I'll try to wake her."

Wendy frowned but stepped aside, motioning for Hook to

help me. I frowned as well but didn't protest, and between the two of us, we managed to get Aife into one of the skin-covered alcoves dug into a wall that functioned as a makeshift bed. I heard Wendy bustling around behind us in the small space, pulling items from the shelves she had hung once after we had been trapped here for a time, surrounded by Nightmares. She had proceeded to deck the place out with supplies, tinctures, and things to help pass the time in case such an occurrence happened again. Since it had only happened once in the decade I had been coming to the Dreamworld, it had annoyed me then—and it annoyed me now.

"I told you, her wounds won't heal," I said over my shoulder as Wendy moved closer, holding a roll of gauze, some salves, and clutching an ewer of water in one hand. "Put that stuff away."

"Maybe *your* brand of healing won't work, but we humans have ways of healing that don't involve magic. I need to clean her wounds and set a dressing so she can start to get better," Wendy replied in a superior tone. "Move over."

"No," I shot back. "*She's* not human, and human efforts won't help her." I turned back to gaze at Aife with renewed wonder. "She's more powerful than she looks," I said reverently, hoping she would wake up soon. "I need her help, and we needed somewhere safe."

"Sounds like she's got you under a spell," Wendy said snidely as I heard her turn and stomp back over to her tidy shelves, her efforts making dust rain down from the ceiling with every step.

I just laughed. "Not exactly. Though if she wanted to spell us all, she could probably do it in a blink." I turned to look at Wendy, who had walked back over with less stomping, and tried to restrain my scowl as Hook stepped behind her silently to look over her shoulder.

"Really? I've never seen you admire someone so much! Are wedding bells finally in the offing? Found someone strong enough to suit your mother *and* yourself?" Wendy asked flippantly. I recoiled at her words.

"Even if I wanted to marry her, I couldn't. I'm already

married."

Wendy blinked, then closed her eyes for a long moment and drew in a steady breath. Hook shifted behind her, raising his hand as if to put it on her shoulder, but after thinking twice, he stepped back to give us room instead.

"I'm sorry, did I hear you say that you're married?"

The grin sweeping over my face stretched my mouth wide as thoughts of my bride swept aside the metaphorical cobwebs of our current situation. "Yes, just a few hours ago, actually."

Wendy cast an appalled look at Aife, and I rolled my eyes. "For the last time, not to *her*. She's a *Shepherd*. And one that's already married, at that. Gross."

"Then who?" Wendy demanded, her eyes flicking back to mine, her expression tight and her dark eyes snapping.

I scoffed. "Why do you care? Did you not just hear me say that we're in the presence of a Shepherd? One of *the* Shepherds? From the beginning of the world?"

"Yes, Peter, my hearing isn't damaged. I asked who you married. Because I don't see anyone else here, but you had a goofy grin on your face when you talked about it. Since I don't see a wife, I'm starting to suspect you're under a spell."

I burst out laughing, clutching my stomach. "I guess you could say I *am* under a spell. A marriage spell!" I sobered up at the memory of Alice, though, and straightened up. "But that's why we're here," I continued, gesturing between myself and Aife. "We got separated from my wife. Aife says I can use the marriage spell to find Alice, but we needed a safe place for her to teach me."

"Alice," Wendy muttered as if trying out the name, then glanced at the slide from the main entrance. "Sounds like someone who wouldn't last five minutes out there by herself."

I sobered even more. "She does have a way of stumbling into scrapes—although to be fair, she has a way of stumbling out of them too. And she has more power than she knows."

Wendy glanced back at me, the familiar sear of jealousy snapping in her eyes. She opened her mouth to say something cutting, but before she could speak, Hook appeared silently at her shoulder again, his eyes burning.

"Did you say Alice?" he asked intently. I scowled at him, disliking his interest.

"I did," I admitted grudgingly.

"Blonde with fair skin? Thin and about five foot six inches?" he asked in a rush, holding his hand to his shoulder to indicate the height.

"I didn't exactly take her measurements when we met, but yes," I answered suspiciously. "You speak as if you've seen her before."

"Oh, not you too?" Wendy cried in disgust, turning on Hook and glaring up at him with her hands on her hips. Their height difference was almost comical, and I had to stifle the sudden urge to laugh, especially as the dark and taciturn Hook was instantly cowed into an apologetic expression.

"*Don't* tell me this Alice is *your* Alice," she demanded.

I did not like the sound of that at all. "She's not *his* Alice. She's *my* Alice," I interjected loudly, stepping toward the two. "Inasmuch as she's anyone's Alice other than her own," I amended quickly, imagining Alice's expression if she could hear our conversation and smiling.

"She's *Princess* Alice," Hook said sternly.

"You married a *princess*?" Wendy shrieked, turning on me and throwing her hands in the air. "After all your sermonizing about avoiding Lily on principle because she's like royalty and sticking it out to find someone down-to-earth?"

"Well, I *am* a sort of prince, after all," I said stiffly."

"*You're* a prince?" Hook said disbelievingly, looking me over in a dismissive way that I found *very* insulting.

"Now, see here—" I started, raising my fists. Before I could get myself into trouble, a thin but powerful voice interrupted us.

"That's probably enough posturing for one day, children," Aife said in an amused tone. "Not that it wasn't entertaining, but I imagine we need to *find* the irrepressible Alice so we can ask her to whom exactly she belongs. And I suppose I could throw my own chip into the pile when it comes to that."

I chuckled, recognizing the same quirk of the eyebrow that Alice had when she was teasing in Aife's expression. Though they looked very different and were separated by countless generations, I could see a family resemblance.

"Are you feeling well enough to teach me?" I asked Aife, walking over to sit on the floor beside her bed. "I was worried our dramatic entrance hurt you badly."

She gave me a brief smile, then winced and put a hand to her forehead. "Well, I've felt better, but I'm awake for now. Come closer."

I scooted within arms reach of her, then sat still again, waiting. Before she could begin, Wendy interrupted us.

"I'm Wendy, by the way, and this is Hook," she said flatly.

"Captain James Hook, at your service, ma'am," the man said smoothly. I turned in my seat to look at him again. He was just standing out of a very practiced bow, which made me dislike him even more. *Wendy accused me of getting together with someone posh, yet here she is, toting around someone like **him** without compunction.* Wendy paid him no mind, examining Aife with suspicion.

"I am Aife, the Red Queen," the Shepherd said, smiling at them. "I'm pleased to make your acquaintance."

I turned back to her, ignoring the others behind me. "Never mind them," I said impatiently. "Help me find Alice. Every second she's up there alone, she's vulnerable."

An amused expression crossed Aife's face, but she held out her hand instead of responding. "Take my hand. It will be easier if I show you."

I did as she instructed, closing my eyes as I took her clammy hand and tried to ignore the wet patches that I knew were drying blood. As soon as I did so, my consciousness zoomed out from under me as if it had suddenly taken flight.

Relax, I heard Aife's voice say. It echoed all around me, and although I was still tense, I tried to stay calm. *I am drawing you into myself—or a tiny part of myself, at least—to show you how to access your marriage bond.*

I tried to pay attention as she sank past her own consciousness, which appeared to me like dancing splashes of light—most of it reddened in raw pain and dark edges. After a time, I thought I could understand what she was doing and considered breaking my connection with her. Before I could, she reached for the thin glowing strand that had rapidly been opening at the back of her mind—or heart, or consciousness, or something in between—and grasped it. A burst of pure violence washed over us, pushing me physically away from her body and drawing a deep gasp from her. When I opened my eyes, it was to see her half lying off the bed, her eyes closed again, but this time her face was contorted in agony.

"Aife?" I cried, hesitating before touching her as I remembered the agony of pain I had felt before breaking contact a moment ago. I ventured to shake her arm, a wave of relief sweeping over me when I wasn't hit with a barrage of pain or sucked back into her consciousness, but my concern grew as she didn't respond to my efforts.

"What happened?" Wendy demanded, stepping forward with dithering hands. "Can we help her? What did you do?"

I pushed away, making a noise of disgust and rising to my feet. "I didn't do anything. She showed me how to find Alice, but when she—" I stopped and swallowed heavily, suddenly feeling as if I had witnessed something intimate and not wanting to divulge the Red Queen's pain to anyone else. "Something happened at the end, something I didn't understand. But I do know how to find my wife."

CHAPTER NINETEEN

Alice

A forest sprang up not far beyond the tower courtyard walls, its silvery beeches casting gloomy shadows that seemed to move in the edges of my vision. The trees were sparse for the first dozen yards, and I walked by several dim little meadows before passing a glade with a perfectly round, still pool in it. I would have simply glanced at it and continued walking—so eager was I to catch up with Peter—but there was the form of a man hovering over the water. That seemed unusual enough to determine whether it was friend or foe before moving on.

I stepped into one of the previously menacing shadows of a nearby tree, which now seemed friendly and protective, and peered over at the man, shifting the book I still carried to one side so I could free one of my arms.

He stood still as a statue, peering down at the stars I could see reflecting in the glass-like pool. I knew instantly that it was the White King. Firstly, he was dressed all in white, and secondly, he had an intricate crown on his brow that held the light of dancing galaxies. Though his skin was dark, there was a ghostly pallor to it, and I realized he was lit by an unusually strong moonbeam. His tall form was strong but fragile somehow. I didn't know whether it was because he was ill or because he was a figure formed by the light—or maybe just a plain old statue of the White King. As I weighed whether he *was* a statue and not a person, he spoke.

When he opened his mouth, he looked straight at me, his eyes piercing my heart with the weight of their wisdom, sadness, and forlorn hope. King though he was and married for longer than this world had existed, he was a man whose closest companion of late was grief, and grief draped itself around him even now—even as he spoke to me.

His words were complete nonsense. *It's worse than the Jabberwocky book,* I thought, then realized that I *could* understand him! It was the same language as the book—the one his Steward had gifted me. I couldn't translate his words—that strange language being what it was—but I could understand his meaning.

He told me a tale of running soldiers, of great armies meeting and clashing, though the object of their fight was unclear. As he spoke, it seemed he was calling the story into being. Figures ran by us, weaving between the trees and dodging here and there, decked in armor and carrying weapons openly. They didn't seem to see us at all.

I have called them, the White King seemed to say. *They come to do battle though I have not called them for that purpose. If they could only hear and understand, they would seek harmony with their enemies and together destroy the Betrayer.*

I wrinkled my brow, trying to understand why he was telling me this. "I—perhaps you shouldn't call them forth, then?" I asked hesitantly.

He shook his head, tension mounting in that oddly young but old face. *It is written in the stars. I dare not disrupt the dance of the heavens and cause further destruction here below. The Lion and the Unicorn are our last hope here—as are you.*

I reared back at his words, then cast a brief look around. Seeing no one, I focused on the king again. *Was he more transparent than before?* "Are you speaking to me?" I asked. When he nodded, I shook my head. "I'm no one's hope. Even if I was, I wouldn't be a last hope."

He smiled, one tinged with sadness. *You have been marked. Anyone can see it, who has eyes. And now you have chosen the path to reclaiming the crown that was forsaken.*

I shook my head more violently. "No, you're mistaken. It's true that I'm trying to get to the last row, and I was told I would become queen, but only because the White Queen asked me to help her sister." I gasped. "Should I find her so I can tell her where you are? It's just—there's something wrong with her. She's not all there, all the time." The king began to shake his head, and I racked my brains to find a way to bring him together with his wife, certain that if they were together, they would be better and more powerful—and able to heal the land and help us avoid doom. "I could run back to the tower to get your steward, Humphrey. I've only just come from there! He's been hoping to see you again—"

He shook his head again, and as he did, it seemed to lose some of its solidity. I could see patches of woodland through him. *He's fading.*

I have seen our meeting coming in the stardance for hundreds of years. I have saved every bit of power I could to speak with you, and I cannot hold this shape very long. Even now, the Queen of Hearts' spells break me apart and send me back to my domain. I have message for you, and for my daughter, if your path crosses hers. Listen to these signs and join the great dance, heart queen: Dreams must die; rifts be healed. Oceans rise; mistakes revealed. Darkness fall; hearts take all.

I muttered the signs back to myself, committing them to memory as the king dwindled.

"But, sire!" I exclaimed, rushing toward him as he became more and more transparent. "There must be a way to keep you here, to reunite you with your queen and your daughter!"

I reached toward him, not daring to step into the starry pool —which reeked of spiky, bright power that I assumed came from his heavenly domain—but my fingers were just out of reach of his person.

He smiled, and for a brief moment, the grief covering him was thrown aside. *"Mistakes revealed,"* was all he said, and then he was gone, leaving me with a shard of grief in my heart that he had spent all his power to come down here and meet with me instead of finding a way to meet with the ones he loved.

Dreams, rifts, oceans, mistakes, darkness, hearts. I repeated. I suppose the meaning will become clear eventually. Add that to the list for when I find Briar—her magic specializes in visions and interpreting them. Perhaps she can interpret a prophecy for me. Right now, I need to be getting on. I hadn't seen soldiers running through the trees in some time, and as the moonlight faded over the pool, the stars reflected in the water went away, and the little glade became gloomy and dark. I drew in a breath and started forward.

The woods thickened as I went along, then thinned again abruptly. Closing my eyes, I tried to use my magical senses to determine what sort of obstacles might be ahead in this row, but the senses that had seemed so delightfully clear back in the garden were still dulled. *Or perhaps it's the Dreamworld itself that feels dull here. It's almost like a muffled headache.* Either way, it was not the same Dreamworld that had dropped a book into my hand when I wanted a picture of the Jabberwocky, or the one that had gotten huffy when I hadn't paid it any attention. *Is it any wonder? It has been soaked in blood for a millenia here, and who knows what horror lies ahead.*

I stopped focusing internally and took a step forward to the edge of the treeline, resting my hand against the rough bark of an oak as I peered out, propping the Steward's book against my hip with my other hand. Ahead of me stretched a vast plain, a gradual slope stretching before me with one final band of trees between me and the river marking the next row, which moved murkily in the distance.

Unfortunately for me, an army—make that *two* armies—with soldiers already clashing in the center of the field, stood between where I was and where I wanted to be. As far as I could see in either direction clashed bands of soldiers, with officers on horseback—and on the backs of great cats and hounds and every other sort of animal you can imagine—rallying those on the front lines. Others moved through the wounded in fits and starts, giving aid or retrieving fallen comrades.

My stomach soured as I scanned the field again, and I shrunk behind the oak tree hoping to avoid the notice of the fighters below. There didn't seem to be a way to avoid crossing the battlefield. There were trees scattered here and there across the plain, though they were more sparse than I would have liked. *Perhaps I can use them as cover. Now I wish I had my dreamwoven blanket-cloak back. Surely it would help keep me hidden.*

A large tent caught my eye as I scanned the battlefield again, its flag flying on a pole high above. Although the sky was as dim as it always was in the Dreamworld, the banner seemed to glow softly of its own accord—a prancing white unicorn on a background of shining silver. I frowned at the flag, something about it stirring my memories. *It's dreamcloth,* I realized with a start. *Just like the blanket I took from Cara's cottage.*

A flap to the tent opened, and a general strode out, barking orders and weaving spells strong enough I could feel her power from where I stood, even though they weren't directed at me. Subconsciously I wove a little protective spell between the general and myself—which backfired spectacularly because it instantly drew her attention. She snapped her head in my direction, piercing me with her gaze. I gasped as I met her eyes.

It was Cara.

"Cara!" I exclaimed, leaving my hiding place and running down the slope toward her, my feet tripping over themselves. I managed *not* to tumble the rest of the way down, weaving my way between little groups of soldiers recuperating near tents and campfires before pulling up short. A cadre of what looked like personal guards had stepped between us, leveling their swords at my throat. I shot an alarmed glance at the Sleep Fairy.

"Let her through," Cara instructed her guards, not missing

even a beat with her spell weaving, "she is no threat to me."

The guards stepped back, their hardened expressions not softening even a little bit, and allowed me to pass. "Cara, what are you doing here?" I asked urgently, "Where is Briar?"

"Stop chattering for a moment and let me finish this," she replied sharply, then turned to the battlefield. I took a few more steps toward her, stopping an arms length away from her elbow. As I did, I felt the spell build to a crescendo and she released it, a physical orb flying from her hands as she thrust them outward. I watched as the orb traced an arc across the field, flying well over the heads of the creatures fighting below, until it seemed to splash against something invisible at the other end, just a few feet away from yet *another* tent. This one was a patchwork of skins and canvas, and the flag flying above it was deep black—so much darker than the gloomy sky that it's jet black color seemed to gleam. Worked on it in a brilliant, burning gold was the image of a lion. Though it was far away, I could make out the snarling features with perfect clarity, and I shivered.

A flap flew open on the patched-together tent, and a man ducked out, standing without fear and immediately looking over at Cara. He smiled, his eyes holding a sort of feral hunger and amusement—and a burning promise of a bloody death. Cara hissed next to me but didn't flinch. *It seems as if she knows him.* The man's eyes turned toward me, and a puzzled expression crossed his face for a moment as he frowned at me. I shrank back, wanting to slink away from the notice of such a being, but he almost immediately lost interest and turned his gaze back to Cara, his grin widening again before turning to duck back into his tent.

I let out a breath when he dropped out of sight. "Who was that?" I asked Cara. "And how could we see him from that far away? Do you know him?"

Cara laughed harshly, then turned to look at me. "Know him? Yes, I know him. I know him as intimately as I know myself, and I hate him with every fiber of my being." I reeled back at her savage words, but she continued on without noticing. "I have fought him countless times over the decades—though not always in battles such as this," she amended, gesturing toward the sprawling field. "It is *his* creatures I have fought at the borders of the Dreamworld which correspond to Spindle, and he has only rarely shown his face. That is how it has ever been between his predecessors and mine—but now he opposes me openly," the frustration in her voice was evident as she cast another glance back at her enemy's tent. "He seeks to overrun the Steward's Tower, so I must tarry here to prevent him, or I would lose control of Spindle's borders." She stopped herself suddenly, looking at me as if seeing me for the first time.

"But you cannot stay, Princess Alice. You shouldn't have come here to begin with, and if I'm honest, I'm surprised you've lasted this long." She gave me an appraising look. "You must have surprising depths of cunning and magecraft. I suppose I shouldn't be surprised that a granddaughter of Queen Corvina would take after her." I answered her approving smile with a timid one of my own. "At any rate," she continued, "now that I've found you, I can take you back to my dark mirror and send you home. The spell I sent against him should prevent him from stepping foot on the battlefield again for some time, but we must go immediately. I can't leave my soldiers undefended for very long."

I shook my head vehemently at her invitation. "No, thank you," I declined, even as my heart wavered with a sudden longing to see home—to feel the sun on my face and have a jam sandwich (*when was the last time I ate?*) and wash it down with a cup tea while my grandmother fussed around me, and my mother gave me a hug and a stern lecture. It was the sort of reception I was used to from my escapades around Dryfaeston, and I longed for my family's familiar embrace.

But that was the reception of a child after a child's adventures. As much as I hoped to see my family again, I had a mission to complete. And though it was less fun with Peter gone from my side, I still had to see it through.

"What do you mean, 'No, thank you'?" Cara demanded,

frowning at me. "I can't risk you being hurt in the battle, and I dare not tempt fate by letting you out of my sight again."

I laughed, amusement suddenly blowing away the smallness and tiredness I had been feeling. "Tempt fate? Now that's an interesting choice of words, Cara," I said with a chuckle. "It seems—strange though it may seem—that my fate lies here, in the Dreamworld. I may have jumped through the mirror impulsively, but I have encountered Shepherds and myths—I have even seen the White Queen and the White King! In fact, I have spoken with their steward, as well," I added, lifting the book I still carried slightly, "and that's just the tip of everything I've experienced. I have a path to walk here—a fate or a doom of my own to meet. I didn't know it before, but the path opening before me has been waiting here for me all along."

Cara blinked at my words—*I don't blame her, I'm not exactly the strong heroine type like The Red Rider*—and seemed to look at me with new eyes.

"Spoken with the steward, you say?" Something twisted in Cara's angular face, but she dismissed the emotion so quickly I thought I imagined it. "Even I have never been allowed to do so during my long years here. What did he tell you?"

I took a breath, suddenly remembering the White King's words. "Many things, but it's what the White King told me that most concerns you. I didn't realize when he said 'the Unicorn,' it would mean *you*, or I would have tried to ask more questions." Cara's eyebrows shot up, "You *spoke* with the White King?! I thought you said you only saw—"

"Yes, yes," I interrupted, eager to press on. "He said he was calling you forth once more and you would go into battle, but it's not for fighting that he called you and your enemy together. If you lay down your weapons you could align to help take down the Betrayer."

Cara barked out a short laugh, pressed a hand to her chest, then let out a long string of laughter that sounded increasingly bitter. I waited patiently until she got herself under control, a sadness seeping into my bones at the weight of years that lay behind her harshness. At last, her laughter faded and she regarded me with resigned determination mingled with pity.

"If I lay down my weapons little Alice, the entire Dreamworld would be overrun by that Lion and his creatures in a heartbeat. It is only the Sleep Fairies who have kept it from happening all this time, and even our number has dwindled until it is only I who can walk here. The White King wants us to lay our weapons down? He would never ask such a thing—you must have been speaking to someone masquerading as the White King." She nodded firmly. "It is just the sort of trick the Lion would play—though how he knew you were connected with me I can't say."

I frowned. "I understand why you wouldn't believe me, having seen the Lion for myself. I don't pretend to know *why* he said it, but that's what the White King told me. And—" I hesitated, wanting her guidance on the king's signs but not wanting her to dismiss them out of hand.

I never got a chance to seek her wisdom, for a great horn trumpeted a call down on the battlefield, and Cara turned her attention there.

"Blast!" she exclaimed, searching the melee below with worried eyes. "Looks like they've rallied a pack of wolves and are pressing a charge. I should have known containing their general would have little effect on the battlefield. They've always been a cobbled-together rabble driven by animal instincts more than leadership."

She barked orders at the officers surrounding her, then returned her attention to me. "Go then, if you believe you have a path to walk. I am not here to babysit princesses, and you are an adult who can make her own choices. When you are done, seek the White Unicorn. I will try to take you home if you can find me again."

I nodded once, my eyes filling with tears as she turned and ran toward the battle, stopping only to mount a noble unicorn that streamed from the forest at her whistle. I turned away, not strong enough to watch such a brilliant and beautiful pair enter the butchery of the melee.

CHAPTER TWENTY

Peter

"Right, because swanning off to find your new girlfriend is more important than helping someone who's clearly suffering right in front of you," Wendy said in disgust as she shooed me away from Aife's side. I scoffed but moved aside, allowing her to sit next to the unresponsive Red Queen and attempt to rouse her. I don't need to defend my relationship with Alice to Wendy. She accuses me of being selfish, but she's just as bad.

Hook flicked his eyes between the two of us but didn't comment. Something itched inside me to snap at him too, but I had bigger fish to fry. Stomping across the room, I settled on the floor—rather awkwardly because of my armor, which didn't help the temper I felt rising inside—with my back against the wall so I could see everyone. It was just a bonus that it placed me as far away from the irritating *Captain* Hook as I could be in the small shelter. Wendy called him over to help her with something at Aife's side, and I watched him go to her before I closed my eyes.

With the world suddenly dark, my other senses leaped to the forefront. I could hear Wendy and Hook murmuring at the other end of the room, though I couldn't *quite* make out their words. Under my legs, the gritty wooden planks of the floor scraped against my armor as I shifted slightly. I breathed in deeply, drawing in the scent of wood and roots and the sort of muffled dirtiness that accompanies things long stored underground. I welcomed and blocked out each of my senses in turn, sinking further into myself, searching for my heart bond. I fumbled and groped, not moving nearly as swiftly or smoothly as the Red Queen had, but in very little time I found myself grinning at a large ray of sunshine that warmed a corner of my heart. *Alice.*

I tried to tug on it like I had seen Aife do, but I couldn't grasp it with my metaphorical hands, or consciousness, or—whatever I was using to find this connection. At a loss, I simply stared at the dancing lights, basking in their warmth and wishing there was an easy way to find Alice.

Gradually, as if fog were clearing in front of my face, I began to see a picture. *Is that Alice?!* It was, I realized, as the image solidified. It felt different than a memory, though I couldn't explain why. At the moment I didn't care. I was happy simply to see her.

At first, I just stared at her face, smiling like a fool. It was clear she couldn't sense me, but seeing her alive and apparently well made me feel as light as a feather. Gradually, the area around her began to fill in, and I started to pay attention, hoping to identify some features that would help me understand where in the Dreamworld she was at the moment—assuming this was real.

She's moving, I realized, *walking through a forest. That could be anywhere*, I griped. *But hopefully, it means she is still in the steward's row.* As I thought it, my field of view widened, and I realized she was just outside the steward's tower, walking into the dense forest beyond. *Aha!* I thought triumphantly. *Now that's what I call a landmark!* As I was basking in triumph, my field of view continued widening. As it did so, I caught sight of a moving shape—several moving shapes. Focusing on them, I realized they were soldiers—dozens, no, hundreds of them. Cold fear struck my heart as I realized they were amassing in a great field directly in Alice's path. Another army was arraying there as well, and I gasped, recognizing the infamous livery of both. *The Lion and the Unicorn have pitched battle—and Alice is about to be caught right in the middle of it.*

With a thump, I landed on the wooden floor and opened my eyes, realizing I had floated off the ground while searching for Alice.

Wendy and Hook had half turned and stared at me with puzzled expressions.

"I found Alice," I explained, desperation creeping into my voice as I pushed off the floor and took a step toward them. "She's in danger! The Lion and the Unicorn are in battle again, and she's heading right toward it!"

Hook's stoic expression seemed to darken considerably. "Where is she?" he demanded. "I'll get her."

I balled my fists at his authoritative tone, anger surging at his assurance that *he* was the best man for the job. "Isn't it your first time here? Even if I told you where she was, you wouldn't be able to find her, *Captain*." I sneered.

"I know if she's heading toward a fight, I'm better able to protect her than you are, *Sir Knight*," the thus far stoic captain sneered back, flicking his eyes up and down my ornately wrought enchanted armor. Every fiber of my being darkened with anger.

"Enough," Wendy cut in, fixing us both with glares. "If she's heading toward the Lion and the Unicorn, she'll need all the help she can get. We'll all go. Once we've got her, we can return here and hope the queen has woken up by then."

I glanced over to where Aife lay, anguish on her sleeping face. "No, you stay with the queen and guard her—in fact, use the safe pathways to get her across the river and into the next row," I told Wendy. She opened her mouth to protest but shut it sullenly as I turned my attention back to Captain Hook. "As for *you*—I suppose I'll take whatever help I can get to keep Alice safe, but you do as *I* say, understand?"

Hook bowed sardonically, and Wendy made a disgusted noise before turning back to the queen.

"Alright then, we'll meet by the Wishing Tree just across the river," I called to Wendy, then motioned Hook to follow me out one of the hideout's exits. "Come on, Captain, let's see if you actually earned that."

Without waiting for his response, I stepped into the recess of another large tree root section, the Captain right on my heels. Wordlessly, I sketched the spell unique to this entrance, starting our rise toward the surface. Crowded together as we were, I couldn't help noticing Hook's height and weight difference. Instead of feeling intimidated, I used the opportunity to size up all the ways I could be faster and more light of foot than he would be. There was no way I'd let him rescue Alice instead of me. *Not that he's outright said he's in love with her, but what other reason would he have for chasing her into the Dreamworld?*

Taking a quick moment to ensure we weren't being observed as we arrived aboveground, I stepped out of the tree trunk. "Keep up and run lightly," I ordered the Captain as I darted forward. "We have a lot of ground to cover, and nothing here will suffer us to pass unscathed."

CHAPTER TWENTY-ONE

Alice

As I fled Cara's tent, I tried to skirt around the battlefield as best I could, flitting from tree to tree and praying they would help me stay hidden from violent eyes.

Fortunately, the meadowland was long rather than wide, and although there was no way to cross it while staying wholly unseen, I wouldn't be exposed for too long. The Steward's book weighed heavily in my arms, and I glanced down, considering what to do with it. After a moment, I untucked the white shirt I was wearing under my waistcoat, then carefully shoved the book up my shirt, tucking my hem back in once I had lodged the book securely inside. With my shirt tucked in, it rested securely between my stomach and my sturdy waistcoat, the edges pressing at me sharply. *It would have to do.* My only other choice was to leave it behind, and I was loathe to do it.

Gathering what little courage I had, I took a breath and started a mad dash as the clash of the battle seemed to reach a fever pitch—my heart racing and lungs gasping as I sprinted for the other side and freedom. The last band of trees before the river reared up in front of me, and I dared not glance around for fear that a look from me would draw the gaze of one of the soldiers. *If I could just get to the first tree—*

I had barely passed the first one when an arm struck out, hitting me right in the chest, knocking the wind out of me and the rest of me off my feet. Dazed and buzzing with fear, I lay frozen on the ground as a dark shape bound my ankles and wrists tightly, then threw me over its shoulder.

My captor walked with an odd gait, my brain noted distantly as I struggled to accept my new circumstances. The shoulder beneath my stomach was muscled and hard, digging in painfully with every jolting step. As my eyes adjusted to my current upside-down predicament, I noticed with a detached fear that my captor skin had scales. *It must be a Beast*, I realized, thinking of the tales my brother had told me of his deployment to the Wasteland. *Somehow one must have wriggled its way through a crack in the Wasteland into the Dreamworld, and now it was going to —*

Canvas and old animal skins brushed over my skin and hair, and suddenly, I was tossed onto a pile of dusty furs, my captor growling something unintelligible before ducking back out of the tent flap through which he had just thrown me.

I glanced around anxiously and immediately noticed one curious thing and one frightening thing. *Or perhaps two things that are both curious and frightening,* my unruly brain noted dispassionately.

Firstly, an enormous lion was seated on its haunches in one corner of the tent. It was ferocious, but had oddly intelligent eyes—and was entirely focused on me. Despite the mind-numbing wave of terror its attention gave me, my eyes wandered to the second curious and frightening thing—a hulking shape seated at a makeshift desk. It was the man Cara had so recently cursed across the battlefield—the one she assured me would be confined to his tent for the time being—and now, apparently, I was going to be confined with him.

He scowled at me, scars marring a savage face that might once have been distinguished. I blinked rapidly, not quite brave enough to scowl back though the sass in my insubordinate brain was beginning to rear its head in response to my dire circumstances. *It's not the time,* I scolded myself in my head. *I'm not an overindulged princess at her grandmother's palace.* The naughty side of my brain noted smugly that I was still an overindulged princess, just in a setting *other* than my grandmother's palace. I cursed it's impudence soundly— promising to write a pretty letter of apology to my governess when I got back home for all the nonsense she endured during my adolescence, whose patience I appreciated more now that I had to endure the nonsense by myself—then flinched as the lion licked it's chops noisily. The man Cara had referred to as the Lion —*did she know there was an actual lion here in the tent with him?*— cleared his throat.

"And who are you, exactly?" he asked in a grizzled voice.

"Oh, well, nobody really," I found myself replying in a reassuring manner that surprised me. *How did those words come to my lips when every bone in my body is shaking? I suppose have an impudent side to one's brain comes in handy in a sticky situation every now and again. The logical side of my brain certainly can't function at the moment.* I glanced between the two other occupants of the tent sullenly. *I'm sure that lion can sense my fear —it does seem rude that animals can do that when we humans can't. They should turn their noses away or something. Not that I'd expect something as magnificent and powerful as* **that** *to worry about manners.*

"I saw you talking to my enemy a few moments ago, didn't I? That means you're Somebody," the man replied stubbornly. "Are you some sort of construct she created to kill me?"

"No!" I replied indignantly, "I'm human." I frowned, then decided since the lion hadn't yet pounced and the man hadn't actually threatened me, I might try and sit upright. They both watched my attempts with obviously increasing amusement— one might ask how the lion expressed its amusement, and I'm sure I don't know, but I could tell it was amused just the same— until finally, the man walked over, drawing dark blade etched in runes from a sheath in his leather boot and cut the bonds around my ankles. His movement was so quick, I only flinched after it was already done, which made him laugh huskily. He went to sit on the edge of his desk while I finally got myself upright, then crossed his arms and considered me thoughtfully.

This whole experience was becoming increasingly confusing. This man was Cara's mortal enemy, at least from what she had said. And although he oozed raw power and looked at thought he had seen and done brutal things with it, he seemed increasingly reasonable. I almost found myself liking him. *That's just that Captor's Syndrome talking,* my impudent part of my brain informed me. It was probably right, but I couldn't help letting my guard down—only slightly!—in his presence.

"I cut your bonds, so it's only right that you give me something in exchange, don't you think?" he asked finally, a smile curving his face. When I just raised my eyebrows at him, he continued on as if I had agreed. "Now, child, what I want to know is why you're important to the Unicorn. I should like to use you against her," he explained in an almost confiding manner, and I found myself inexplicably wanting to help him, despite the fact that he was Cara's enemy.

"Well, I'm nothing much to her, really," I answered truthfully, though somehow having the presence of mind to avoid confiding that I was a princess. "She's my friend's godmother." I frowned, trying to remember properly. "No, that's not right, she's *not* my friend's godmother, which I think was the whole point behind why we ran to her to begin with—" I shook my head, confusing myself. "Anyway, the Unicorn said she didn't have time to babysit me, so I'd have to find her again later. Please don't use me against her," I added belatedly, keeping my tone polite and carefully not looking at the lion, who, at this moment, settled down onto his forepaws—though he continued his examination of me.

"Hmm...well, she very definitely let me see you with her, so she has some cunning plan, I'm sure. She always does, that one. I'm sure she wants to use *you* against *me* in some way." He looked over at the lion. "She does think she's smarter than us, doesn't she?" he asked him. The lion yawned widely, then snapped his mouth closed and ambled to his feet.

"Stay here," he ordered me, then returned to his conversation with the lion. "It's time we showed her how effective her spells are when it comes down to brute strength, don't you think?"

A bewildering moment later, I was left alone in the tent. He hadn't even bothered to put a spell on me to keep me in place. *He must be very sure that I can't escape.* Still, since there were no magical bonds keeping me in place, I decided to test my mediocre running skills against any guards he had stationed at the entrance of his headquarters. I wavered only long enough to draw in a deep breath—which I regretted instantly since the tent was musky and full of dust—and ran out the way I had entered.

The noise of battle instantly assaulted me, though I couldn't see it from behind the tent. There must have been some sort of noise-reducing spell on it because the overwhelming cacophony of clashing steel and screeching cries threatened to send me back into the tent for a little of the muted silence that had been inside. Instead, inexplicably finding the entrance unguarded, I willed myself onward and toward the nearby line of trees. I couldn't avoid passing several beastly creatures as I ran, but they paid me little heed. I ignored them right back on the premise that confidence might carry me through where skill in a fight would not. It obviously worked because in a few minutes I was deep in the woods, and although I could still hear the sounds of battle, they were far off now and felt as if they had nothing to do with me.

How can Cara face such grisly work? I wondered. Although *her* body was in the physical world, would she die if she were killed here in the Dreamworld? I didn't know enough about spirit walking to understand the risks she was taking, but even if she wouldn't die, surely she carried lifetimes of horrors in her spirit.

"No wonder she seems crabby all the time," I muttered to myself, wiping a bead of sweat from my forehead.

As I took a moment to get my bearings and my breathing under control, I began to notice that the woodland around me felt very dark. It *looked* dark, too—in the way that dense forest can even at midday—even though it wasn't nightfall. *Does nightfall ever happen here in the Dreamworld?* I couldn't help my wayward curiosity wandering even as I sensed danger rising around me. I wished desperately for a sign or a pathway from the Dreamworld, but like the other side of this row, the playful Dreamworld I had sensed earlier in my adventure was a stranger to me. *And maybe it's best that I'm not connecting with it now*, I realized with a shiver. If it was ornery at its best moments, there's no telling how it would interact with me while a battle was raging.

I wondered if that was the reason I felt so unsettled by my surroundings, but decided after a moment that it was the fact that there was no birdsong. I slowed my breathing until I was completely silent, listening carefully, but there was nothing. *Not that there was birdsong in most places here, but in the woods, you expect it.* It reminded me of the Wood of Forgetting. *If I have to cross another one, I don't know how I'll reach the other side by mself.*

"Perhaps there just aren't any birds living in this particular wood," I told myself bracingly, scanning the trees quickly to try and find some sort of path. Thus far there had always been a path—a clear way forward. Now there was nothing. *And everything is so still. No birds winging this way and that, rustling leaves as they take flight. No squirrels or chipmunks making branches jump as they leap from tree to tree.* I swallowed heavily. I wanted out of this woodland with every fiber of my being.

"Better just go then," I ordered myself, stepping around a beech tree and wincing with each crunch my footsteps made on the bed of dead leaves and twigs covering the forest floor. I crept along as best I could, following a slight rise in the ground, hoping if it rose high enough, I could see the boundary river, which should be *very* close now.

The ground began to turn rocky rather than leaf-strewn, although the trees didn't seem to thin out. *The last strip of trees didn't seem that wide from across the battlefield. I hope I'm not going sideways down the row rather than across!* Great jagged boulders stuck out of the ground, and I tried to step from rock to rock to avoid the crunching gravel between. I didn't think there were soldiers this far from the battle, but I didn't want to attract the notice of anything else in this row, soldier or not. After one such leap, I froze, my growing fear becoming tangible in an instant. A chanting murmur reached my ears—there were others nearby.

As the chanting rose and fell, murmuring eerily in the distance, my courage seemed to rise and fall with it, leaving my heart filled with waves of fear and deep and dark undefinable horrors. I wanted nothing more than to get away from this forsaken woodland, but I dared not move. *What's the use of having an affinity with this Dreamworld, if I can't use it when I'm in danger? If I can control it, shouldn't I be able to fight its inhabitants or improve its rows?* Even though I was more afraid than I'd ever been, there was a tiny bit of outrage in my heart—the merest grain of sand—that chafed at the darkness in this world when it could be filled with light.

"And, after all," I whispered, hoping that speaking out loud would bolster my tiny seed of courage against the fear that overwhelmed me, "why should a bit of singing stop me from moving to the next row? Peter and Aife are probably waiting for me. It can't be far now."

I drew in a fortifying breath and took a few halting steps, peering around the next boulder in the direction of the chanting, which suddenly grew louder.

I immediately regretted it. There, in a stone circle only a few yards away, were the same creatures Peter and I had seen in the garden so long ago. They looked up at the sound of my footsteps, and their eyes gleamed. They had seen me, and they were calling the Jabberwocky.

Instantly, I broke into a run, and just as quickly bounced off of a boulder. But it wasn't a rock; it was a huge, troll-like creature straight from one of my fairytale books at home. Its stench was overwhelming, nearly as powerful as its strength—which was unfortunately all too apparent as it picked me up like a child, tucking me under one arm as if I were a bundle of clothes and bellowing to its comrades as it started toward the circle.

A gibbering screech echoed on the rocks as the malformed creatures hooted and cackled triumphantly at my capture. Whatever they had planned for me couldn't be good, and the fear that had threatened to drown me as I crouched among the stones wormed its way into my bones, threading itself in every sinew of my muscles, rushing along my bloodstream as if it were ice water.

The troll stomped into the stone circle and dropped me unceremoniously onto a roughhewn boulder in the middle. A fresh wave of terror flooded my body as some part of my brain noticed the similarity of this boulder with the one on which we found Aife not long ago. She had been in a sunny meadow with horrible grass and flowers thriving on her blood, not a barren, rocky stone circle like this one. *Maybe her meadow started as rocky and barren as this place, and her blood nourished its changes over the centuries.* Horror at the thought rose out of my throat in the form of a strangled cry. A detached part of my brain reminded me I wouldn't have to worry about that since I wouldn't live for centuries. It wasn't very comforting.

Maybe I can change this place like I changed my clothes earlier if I try hard enough. Or perhaps I can change where I am using my connection to the Dreamworld. I squeezed my eyes shut, and as I did, the chanting swelled in power. I felt it like a shackle on my wrist, the accompanying power and fear like a barrier to my mind. Panic took me, and I gasped for air, opening my eyes as a dark shimmer started flickering in the air.

They were finishing summoning the Jabberwocky, and I would be the first thing it saw. *And it will be the last thing I see.*

CHAPTER TWENTY-TWO

Peter

With each step, my feet wanted to leap into the air instead of running. I want to soar over these trees, find Alice, and swoop down to save her. But if I did that, especially in this row, I would attract any flying Nightmare within leagues—not to mention the attention of the soldiers currently fighting for the Lion and the Unicorn. A flying Nightmare I could probably defeat, although not without injury. Two armies of soldiers dedicated to death and destruction? Not a chance.

Hook hustled along behind me, staying annoyingly quick and quiet. My dislike of the man grew with every moment. He was too professional, too dangerous, and too focused on Alice. Although I would welcome any help he could give me, I didn't trust him further than I could throw him. Which wouldn't be very far if I was honest.

Still, although I didn't dare use pixie dust to fly to my Alice, I did use my own magic to speed my steps, leaping lightly so I made no noise as I crossed the carpet of dry leaves which gradually gave way to gravel and rocks. I had crossed this way once before, but it was many years ago, and all I remembered was that it was a barren part of the forest with scrubby pines and rocky boulders. If what I had seen of Alice had been correct, she would be heading this way, and I should cross her path soon enough.

A whisper to our left was the only warning that something shared the woods with us. Diving sideways, I rolled over my shoulder and ducked behind a tree as I came up again, just in time to watch Hook plunge his sword into the neck of a horrifying Nightmare. This particular creature was so twisted beyond recognition that I couldn't tell what it once was. Simply a collection of gnashing teeth and sharp hooves. It had fur rather than armor or scales, which accounted for the swift dispatch Hook had achieved. Still, as grateful as I was that the creature was dead, it irked me that *he* had been the one to do it.

"I could have dispatched it with a spell," I said as I stepped back out from behind the tree. "Less mess that way."

"Indeed," was Hook's only reply as he released a cleaning spell over his sword and slid it back into its scabbard. His tone had been mild, but I couldn't help but see reproof and superiority in his eyes as he motioned us forward again. Barely restraining myself from snarling at the challenge, I followed his unspoken order and bounded off, my fear for Alice growing with every step we took. I could only hope her affinity for the Dreamworld's innate magic would help her best a Nightmare if she came across one before I reached her.

Reaching a series of boulders that I suddenly recognized as the highest point around this patch of woodland, I leaped onto the first one, reaching the largest one with a couple more jumps before stopping to balance on the edge. Hook had kept running for a few steps on the ground below before realizing what I had done. Instead of following me up, he stood back and tipped his head back to look at me.

"Can you see her?" he demanded, watching me closely. I ignored him as I scanned what little I could see of the woodland around us, then slowed as I came to a slightly more open area ahead, the trees interspaced with a field of boulders that increased in density before petering off into a band of forest that I knew butted up against the river marking the end of this row. Hook muttered to himself below, turning his back to me and scanning the trees nearby with his sword drawn.

As I searched methodically through the dim vista, a creeping dread fluttered around the edges of my mind. My own brand of faerie magic, stemming from a connection to an island that, despite its faults, was largely free of evil, tended to keep away the creeping dread that seemed to affect other visitors to the Dreamworld, especially in this particular row. Wendy needed a lot of pixie dust to keep it away when we were here, but I hadn't felt this sort of fear unless I was—

I sucked in a sharp breath, my eyes having found the source of the uneasiness that flitted around my mind and was clearly affecting Captain Hook below. A collection of motley creatures had gathered near an old stone circle amongst the boulders, the ancient worked rocks more than half tumbled down into ruin. Their chants were barely audible, but I recognized those motions —they were calling the Jabberwocky. Wasting no time, I leaped down the rocks until I was on level ground with Hook again, my mind racing. We had to get to Alice, but I would need Hook's fighting experience if I wanted us all to survive.

"Did you see her?" Hook demanded, flicking a glance my way before turning to scan our surroundings again, the scowl on his face the only betrayal that the fear produced by the Jabberwocky's summoning was affecting him.

"No, but I did see something bad," I answered, then nodded to myself as I came to a decision. "There are creatures summoning a great evil just ahead. I'm hoping we can skirt around that place, but I don't want to wander too far in case Alice stumbles upon them. She was heading this way in my vision."

"Then lead on," Hook said stoutly, even as some of the color drained from his face.

I shook my head. "First, I need to give you armor like mine," I insisted, indicating my now pristine white knight's armor. The spell that created it had cleaned it, and although I had worn it when I entered the Dreamland as more of a costume than anything else, it functioned as actual armor, and contained numerous protective spells that just might help us both survive an encounter with the Jabberwocky. *I should have insisted that Alice let me give her a set of armor earlier.*

Hook cast a skeptical look at my armor. "I can sense that it's magically forged, but I'll trust my own armor, thank you."

I repressed the urge to snort as I glanced at the dark leather jerkin peeking out under his uniform. I could sense several layers of excellently crafted spells on it, but none that would withstand the strange magic of the Dreamworld for long—especially if the Jabberwocky arrived.

"You won't need to remove your armor, but believe me when I say you'll need additional protection if the creature they're summoning arrives. It will only take me a minute to do."

Hook stared at me with narrowed eyes for a moment, then shrugged and went back to scanning our surroundings. "Fine, if it means we can keep moving."

I nodded, pulling a knife from my weapon's belt and stepping forward to swiftly cut a lock of his hair. He jerked away and brought the tip of his blade up between us. "It's for the spell!" I protested, holding my hands up. He glared at me for a moment, then went back to his self-imposed sentry duty.

As I promised, it only took a moment to formulate the magical armor, and I cast it on him with a whisper of power that I hoped wouldn't attract any unwanted attention nearby. The familiar sight of magically created armor began encasing Hook from the feet up.

I frowned a moment later, as instead of the brilliant white of my own armor, I realized that Hook's was a dark crimson. He held up his arm as the armor flowed over it, examining the magic with a frown. "Why did you make it red?" he asked.

I shook my head and held up my hands. "I didn't!" I exclaimed, flicking back through the elements of the spell in my mind. "I did the same thing I always do, and mine is *always* white!"

"Are you trying to make me stand out?" Hook growled, taking

a menacing step closer. I didn't back up, but the anger in his eyes made me pause before spitting back with my usual brand of sarcasm.

"No," I protested, running through the spell once more in my mind. "The only thing different from how I usually do it is that I used a lock of *your* hair instead of mine." I looked back over his armor thoughtfully. "I guess I've never cast that spell on anyone else, now that I think of it. Maybe everyone has a different color armor."

Hook grunted, and although he didn't seem completely satisfied with my answer, he shrugged his shoulders as if trying to settle the armor, and my answer, more comfortably. "Let's go, then," he ordered, stepping back to let me lead the way once more.

We had only been running for a few more minutes when the sounds of chanting became audible. The building power in the spell caused a shiver down my spine, and I heard Hook's footsteps falter behind me for a second. A moment later, we both stuttered to a stop when a wordless scream went up. It was Alice.

CHAPTER TWENTY-THREE

Alice

Shimmering darkness flickered above my head. How can darkness shimmer? that distant corner of my mind wondered, still somehow unaffected by the fear paralyzing the rest of my mind and body. Perhaps it's not really shimmering, and I'm so overwhelmed by fear that my eyes are trying to manifest something physical.

The darkness continued shimmering, and despite my attempts to convince myself it was all in my head, the creatures chanting followed it with their eyes as it coalesced into ribbons—ribbons that began to weave themselves in and out of the broken standing stones. Their movement was almost hypnotic. To be sure, I was still stiff with fear and horror, but my eyes couldn't seem to help trying to find a pattern in the weave.

There was no pattern to be found by my muddled mind. If the weavers of this spell tried their hand at knitting or weaving cloth, they would never turn a profit. The dark threads dipped in and out and around the stones, doubling back without a care for the stitch they might have made, twisting with other threads haphazardly and twining around and around seemingly random stumps of stone.

A sudden pressure swept out from the darkness, rippling through the threads and casting the chanting creatures onto the ground. Their chanting continued, although the strain was evident in their voices. It pressed me back into the stone, as the Steward's book—which had somehow managed to stay in place under my shirt all this time—pressed into my lungs. The jagged stone beneath me pricked my back and the distant, still-lucid part of my mind noted that I would need to clean any cuts thoroughly with soap when this was all over. That voice sounded suspiciously like my mother's.

It's nice to know your mother's anxieties follow you even unto a certain death scenario in the Dreamworld. Perhaps my children would remember my injunctions to mind their manners and keep their posture straight during the fight of *their* life someday. Not that Peter would probably want children—or that I wanted them any time soon. Still, if we had them, I hope they had his green eyes. *Green like growing things,* I mused, then snapped back to reality as the invisible force pinning me to the rock snapped back on itself, lifting me several inches off the rock before gravity caught me and slammed me back down.

"Ow," my voice muttered, surprising my brain with its forwardness. *Surely it's not the done thing to voice your pain when facing your death. In my defense, I don't think my governess covered that during lessons.*

A roar louder than any noise I had ever heard—or indeed felt, as it reverberated through my chest with enough force to make me cough—trumpeted from a few yards away. My eyes widened as they were drawn to the source of it.

A dragon. Not just any dragon, the Jabberwocky, as Peter had named it. As horrible as it had been from afar, its skeletal frame seemed massive this close—all sharp edges and claws. Its leathery skin looked rough and thick as armor.

*You **stink** of the Red Queen,* it thought into my mind, an image of myself as I must appear lying on the rock accompanying the words. I looked small and pathetic; my skin was white as paper—or Peter's armor. The fear that had been assaulting me since I had stumbled into the spellcasters suddenly floated away with that image. I was so utterly defenseless in this creature's mind, and his malice so pervasive in his words and thoughts—in his very presence—there was no longer any fear that I would die tonight, only knowledge. And with that knowledge, I felt peace.

Perhaps, I thought to myself as I blinked at the scarred and twisted creature looming over me, *perhaps this was the path the White Queen asked of me all along, and why she seemed so sad to ask it of me. Perhaps my death was written in the stars in this place, and that's why the White King wasted his last strength to send me to it. After all, the Red Queen is my foremother, and she has bled for us for a thousand years. Perhaps my blood will stop hers, and with her power restored, she can bring balance back to the world—call the other Shepherds forth and reshape it as it was meant to be.*

The thought that I might be meant to walk this path wasn't very comforting, but it did give me a curiosity about what my last few moments might mean to the wider world. I frowned at the Jabberwocky, which seemed to be sniffing at me with its wicked maw, and I suddenly wondered at its intelligence. *A beast that has become intelligent? Perhaps this is the one that is organizing the others in the Wasteland.* I looked at it with fresh eyes and thought I saw something more. Not something visible, but a hidden part of this monster that felt familiar. Almost human. My mouth raised in a smile. Persinette would say how like me it would be to try and find some common ground with a monster. I would miss her. I would miss my whole family, and felt sorrow for the sadness I knew they would as they grieved for me.

Peter would grieve for me too, I thought suddenly. I had been uncertain whether he could settle into a full partnership with me, but now it was as if all the puzzle pieces had fallen into place. He wouldn't have to settle because I wasn't a very settled person. I liked to create routines, and I loved finding friends and new family everywhere, but I was curious enough to join his adventures and invite him into mine. He would never force me into a cage because he hated the thought of them himself. And I would never make him change who he was. We could have lived a life of adventure and laughter together. *Maybe raised a pack of feral children together at some point. Neverland sounded like a perfect place for it.*

I sighed, which seemed to get the Jabberwocky's attention.

You stink of the traitor's blood. **Where is she?** He demanded, a wave of magical compulsion accompanying his words. I opened my mouth to reply automatically but then closed it again.

I don't actually know at the moment, I thought back politely instead, since it seemed to be his preferred method of communication. *But even if I did, I wouldn't tell you,* I added firmly. *You would certainly hurt her, and she's been hurt enough.*

The Jabberwocky trumpeted his rage, the sound shaking the air even as his stomping feet made the ground tremble, loosening boulders and sending bursts of dirt into the air.

Then I will take what I want from your mind, he raged at me, and I felt a shocking crack as if a great sledgehammer hit my mind. The first blow was excruciating, and I shrunk away from it, putting a great distance between my thoughts and his assault, which seemed to enrage him based on the continued trumpeting and stamping. He even went so far as to sweep out his great wings as if to take off. Unfortunately for him, I wasn't interested in having a battle in my own mind, so I simply ignored him.

It won't be long now, I mused as I watched his increasingly frantic movements. It was strange to be ending my days as a martyr. Only a month ago, I was campaigning for permission from my parents and grandmother to go off to Deerbold to visit my brother as if it were the height of a grand adventure. *It was a nice change from all the royal balls. How surprised old me would have been if she had known where that journey would end. I suppose I should take some time now to wish I was back at those interminable balls instead of here, but they really were intolerable.*

The mental assault stopped suddenly, and the Jabberwocky seemed to gather itself. *Here it comes—this will be it, I expect. I feel as if I should be doing something now. I'm afraid I'm not making a very good martyr. I'm sure I should be making a speech or trying valiantly to do* **something**, *but I'm quite unable to move, and the* *only thing on my mind right now is what could have been with Peter, which seems a bit off-topic to heroic martyrdom. I should probably be thinking lovingly of all the people my death might serve, but since I actually have no idea what's going on half the time I just can't picture it. It **is** wretched to realize you're a second-rate martyr. Still, I suppose they'll spice it up in the history books for me.*

The Jabberwocky swept out his great wings and beat them once, twice, three times to raise himself into the air—and then he dove.

CHAPTER TWENTY-FOUR

Peter

Alice's scream seared my soul. The sound was excruciating, and I wanted to whisk her away and make it stop—make it so that sound never left her mouth again. I pushed my magic into every step I took, going faster and faster, my armor scraping against rocks and tree trunks and I still felt as if I were moving as slow as molasses toward Alice and the great darkness gathering where I had last seen her.

A muted thwack sounded from ahead and off to my left. I spared a startled glance in that direction, only to be more surprised as I watched a twisted beast crumple to the ground with a knife sticking out of its eye, its body skidding for several feet as momentum carried it when its legs no longer could.

"Keep moving," Hook ordered behind me. "I'll keep them at bay, but we must get to Alice."

"I know," I shot back irritably, hating that my tone somehow sounded like I was a petulant boy instead of a man as capable as he. It was especially irritating since he was a trained—*highly trained, apparently*—soldier. As I had only ever participated in the carefully curated fights between the pirates and the faeries on Neverland, I had never needed serious combat training. In the Dreamworld, magic and trickery were the surest defense against lurking monsters, as long as one was careful to stay out of sight. Now I was rushing headlong toward the most dangerous creature that roamed this land, and I wished I had more skills to defend Alice.

Hook took out two more creatures—one with wings which raked my helm as it dove at us—before we came in sight of the stone circle. A ring of Beasts stood still amongst the stones, watching with mixed horror and glee as the Jabberwocky drew itself up. A small, pale figure lay on the jagged stone in the middle—a calm, almost thoughtful, expression on her face. *Alice.*

"I'll make a hole, and you use your flight magic to get her out of there," Hook ordered, drawing alongside me in ground-eating steps and holding a sword that emanated power and death. He didn't wait for my response, overtaking me in another leap and clashing with the first of the Beasts. By the time I caught up, he had indeed made a hole in their line, having dispatched three and then a fourth as I stepped through. He worked silently, the jabbering of the others drowned out by the continued screeching and groaning of their comrades around the circle, who had not yet noticed us.

Even as I stepped through, the Jabberwocky rose into the air, beating its horrible wings once, twice, three times, as it rose above Alice. Throwing caution to the wind, I reached into my pocket for a pinch of pixie dust, threw it over myself, and dove for Alice just as the Jabberwocky did the same.

The stench of the dragon was overpowering, and I strained with every part of my being to reach Alice—who still hadn't seen me—before it did. Everything came down to reaching her; nothing else mattered. Not if I was hurt or even died, not if I put myself in harm's way, not anything except saving Alice.

My wings burst from my back as I flew, startling me but giving me a jolt of speed that pushed me ahead of the Jabberwocky. I flicked the last of the pixie dust over Alice as I surged toward her—hoping to break whatever enchantments were holding her there—then scooped her into my arms in the next moment. Her startled gasp was quickly drowned out by the snap of teeth and a roar of rage.

"You have wings!" she breathed in my ear, clutching my neck as she huddled in my arms.

I laughed, delighted that amongst all the horror, she was fascinated with my wings. I craned my neck to see where the Jabberwocky was while we rose above the heads of the creatures below. With a trickle of fear, I noticed his enormous neck swinging in our direction. Usually, my powers of flight—especially fast with my newly emerged wings—meant immediate escape from danger. But our foe was not bound to the ground as most were. He was so enormous he hadn't even left the ground yet, but his dangerous maw was level with us still. He opened his mouth, and I feared to find out if the legends were true about the fire in their breath when Hook shouted, "Here!" from down below.

I glanced down to see him crouched on the rock from which I had lately stolen Alice, a grim, deep crimson figure full of quietly controlled violence. His presence was directly at odds with the Jabberwocky's loudly chaotic one and he was focused entirely on the dragon. Hook's intention flashed into my mind, and I instantly stopped beating my wings, tightening my arms at Alice's surprised yelp and turning our sudden free-fall into an angled dive that the Jabberwocky followed eagerly.

As we rushed by the rock, I aimed for the ground in front of it, landing on my feet in an awkward stumbling run, but keeping my balance and holding on to Alice securely. I ran, then leaped into the air again off of another low rock. Behind me, I heard a clash of steel on bone, and a thunderous roar shook the Dreamworld and everything in it, the vibration in the air rippling through my wings painfully.

You DARE strike me with one of my own swords?! the Jabberwocky's voice demanded in an agonizingly loud mental shout. I glanced back and saw that the dragon focused on Hook now, myself and Alice forgotten for the moment as it shook its head, attempting to dislodge Hook from where he hung on its snout, still clutching his great sword, which was currently lodged in its eye.

As I watched, the sword slid free, and Hook slithered down the dragon's face, dangerously close to its gnashing teeth, only to land with impossible grace on the ground below amidst steaming drops of dragon blood.

"Save him!" Alice urged, but I shook my head and angled away from the fight, pouring on as much speed as I could manage.

"I can only save one of you, and I'll always choose you, Alice," I said firmly. At her choked sob, I forced myself to feel a little sympathy for the soldier below. "He's as competent and deadly a soldier as I've ever seen, and he bears a dragon-made sword, apparently. He stands a better chance than any other mortal to escape with his life," I tried to reassure her.

She merely tightened her arms around my neck and sobbed. I kissed her forehead soothingly, then concentrated on covering our flight as best I could, and searching for signs of Wendy and Aife as we neared the stream separating the next row.

I spotted them only moments later, Aife resting with her closed eyes against an the enormous trunk of the Wishing Tree, while Wendy stood guard in front of her with a frown. *We really were close to the next row,* I realized, wishing everything that had happened in the Steward's row could have been avoided. If only we had landed in a slightly different place...I shook my head. No use looking back. *We need to get down there and move to a more secure location.* The instant the Jabberwocky finished with Hook, it would come winging after us, and if I could find Aife and Wendy so easily, so would he.

I angled my descent toward them, shivering as we passed a band of cold air above the river, then came to a gentle landing a few feet away from Wendy. Her eyes passed over us quickly as if checking to ensure we were alright, and then she gave me a nod.

"So this is Alice?" she asked, tipping her chin to my wife, who was still hiding her tears in my neck.

I nodded but didn't make introductions. They could wait

until Alice felt ready and we were in a safer place.

"Where's Hook?" she demanded, turning to scan the opposite bank, her hands on her hips.

"He didn't make it," I admitted. "We ran into *it* when we were getting Alice, and he stayed to distract it so we could escape." Alice shuddered at my words, then went quiet, drawing into herself as she seemed to do when she was overwhelmed.

"What?!" Wendy demanded, turning on me. "You left him behind? How could you! Of all the cowardly—"

"Cowardly?" I shouted back, a spike of anger overtaking my desire to get us moving for the moment. "You have no idea what you're talking about. It was a near thing back there, and I barely escaped with Alice. Hook suggested the distraction in the first place, and he knew the risks. Take it back, Wendy, or you're no friend of mine."

"Oh really?" Wendy sneered, balling her fists at her side and stepping closer. "Is that supposed to make me quiver with sorrow?! I don't make friends with cowards, so if you don't fly back now with those fancy new wings I see you've got, and retrieve Hook, I'll drag you back by your ear—and we *still* won't be friends."

"He wouldn't want us to go back into danger," came Alice's quiet voice. I angled my face to look at her, and she patted my chest before stepping out of my embrace to face Wendy. I snagged her hand as she did so, earning a tremulous smile from Alice and a seething grimace from Wendy.

"Ah yes, the magnificent Alice," Wendy spat, crossing her arms and looking my wife up and down insolently. "The reason Hook came to this accursed place, to begin with, and for whom he has lost his life in apparent devotion." She nodded at our joined hands, "Misplaced devotion from the looks of it. Betraying his life wasn't enough, was it?" Wendy accused. "You had to betray his heart with another as well." Her misinformed words drew a wave of ire from the depths of my soul like I had never felt before. I took a menacing step forward before another voice broke in.

"It's not like that, Wendy," Hook's baritone interjected, and we turned as one to watch the dripping wet and bloodied Captain Hook emerge from the river clutching his arm to his chest, his armor torn.

"Hook!" Alice exclaimed, dropping my hand and rushing to hug the other man. The sight sent a spear of jealousy right through my heart as I watched him gingerly move his injured arm out of the way to accept her affection. Even as his good arm patted her back, his eyes never left Wendy, who glared at them with an edge of anger that curiously seemed to provoke a flash of amusement on Hook's face, almost too quickly to be seen. The sight made me dislike him even more. He held my wife in his arms and seemed to have a connection with my best friend that I didn't understand. *Although I don't think I can be best friends with her anymore. She has too much ire toward Alice, and her jealousy and single-mindedness have pushed me away for years.* Her accusation of cowardice still wrankled. Now that I thought about it, I couldn't remember the last time our friendship had felt easy. *I don't really understand her, and she doesn't understand me,* I realized suddenly. *I don't know that I ever did, actually.*

I watched as Alice stepped out of Hook's embrace and moved back toward me with a weary smile on her face. "Oh I forgot!" she exclaimed suddenly, then inexplicably started untucking her shirt. I watched with increasing amusement as she did a wriggling sort of dance, then pulled a book out from under her waistcoat. "This book came into my possession after you left. Could you put it in that hand bag you have?" she asked sweetly. I opened my mouth to question her further, but just shook my head instead, a smile curving my lips as well. *I can ask later,* I thought as I opened the satchel at my waist and shoved the book inside. A glance at the title revealed nothing, since it was in a language I didn't know, but that hardly mattered at the moment. *I'm glad I included that bag with my armor.* Alice's propensity for collecting random objects was endearing. *I'll have to clear out an entire room at home if she keeps collecting things at this rate.* She claimed my hand when she reached my side, and feeling of wholeness settled on me, visions of our future dancing in my mind.

"We need to move," Hook ordered the company at large, disrupting my revelatory thoughts.

"Can you carry her?" Alice asked me, motioning toward the Shepherd, who hadn't stirred or opened her eyes during our shouting.

Before I could respond, Hook stepped past us and crouched at Aife's side, pulling her across one of his still-armored shoulders with his good arm, then lifting her in an easy motion. "Let's move," he ordered again. "Every second we stay here, we put ourselves in danger. The Jabberwocky is not dead, but I have angered him beyond all reason, and he will find me if he can, to take revenge for the eye I ruined."

He turned and swept into the trees at a swift pace, Wendy following without a word. I pushed down the irritation I felt at his words, which carried a tone of censure to my ears, as if I hadn't intended to do the same exact thing when I had found Aife and Wendy but had been delayed by the apparently inaccurate news of his death.

Alice tried to keep up but was soon dragging at my hand, whatever ordeals she had suffered having drained her strength. Without asking, I pulled her into my arms, unable to use my wings to fly her in the dense woodland, but drawing on my magic to give me strength to carry her. She didn't protest; she simply laid her head on my shoulder.

As I had expected, Wendy must have directed Hook to one of the nearby safe spots we knew of in this row, considering we took a path straight to it. Hook was already setting Aife down and casting a cloaking spell on her as I stepped into the small sheltered clearing covered by large oak boughs from above.

He stood, glancing at Wendy before seemingly drawing a mask over his face and bowing at my wife as she stepped out of my arms again.

"Lady Alice," he said formally, "I have been sent here to retrieve you, and thank the Creator, I have somehow found you.

I'll give you a few moments to say your goodbyes, and then we will leave to seek a way home."

I stepped up next to Alice, opening my mouth to give Hook a piece of my mind, but Alice sensed my intention and put a gentle hand on my arm.

"Captain Hook, you have done well, and I cannot thank you enough for discharging your duty so admirably. My plans, however, have changed. I have no pressing duties at home, as you well know. But I do have new ones here, and a new life." Her hand tightened on my arm, and she gave a delighted little laugh, the sound brightening the gloomy space where we stood in a little knot, Aife a shadowed figure off to the side. "You have the honor of being the first Spindalian to meet my new husband, Peter. I know it is a shock," she said soothingly as if in response to some expression she saw on his face of stone, "but we are vowed to each other, and it cannot be broken. I will remain here and complete the course I have started in the Dreamworld. I release you from your vow of protection over me, and if you so choose, you may return home with news of me. I will send word to my family when I can, but I have much to do."

Hook absorbed this news without betraying a single emotion to my eyes, though Alice obviously saw something in his face, as she stiffened beside me.

"A vow of protection?" Wendy asked suddenly, addressing Hook.

"I am Princess Alice's bodyguard," he replied, flicking a glance at her. "Or was, until she released me from my vow just now. But I have a duty to the crown, not just to you," he said, turning back to Alice. "I was charged to bring you back, and I'll have to fulfill that duty—even if you don't wish to go."

"You don't understand," Alice protested. "I have a mission here—"

"Milady, respectfully, *you* don't understand. You're playing a game with thoe of power that you can't comprehend. I barely escaped with my life back there, and I'm one of the highest-trained warriors in the royal guards. That *dragon* was not just a mere beast—it spoke to me! It claimed to be the maker of my sword, which, as you know, is a guardsman's sword—made by the Red King himself. If that was truly him, he has turned into something dreadful, and his power and hatred will destroy us all if we remain here."

"Hook, I know—" Alice started, but the Captain interrupted her protest.

"That person," he pointed toward Aife, "is the Red Queen, or so I've been told. She has been wounded so badly that she won't even wake. The horrors that caused such wounds to a *Shepherd* are too much for you, or any of us! This is not a debate. We must go." He took a step toward us, but I stepped in front of Alice, and he stopped short.

"I believe you misheard the lady," I said tightly. "She wants to stay."

"And I said I have a duty," he answered through clenched teeth, casting another almost apologetic glance at Wendy. "No matter what any of us might want, I will be taking her home."

"My home is here," Alice said firmly, stepping out to stand at my side again, "with Peter. And I *do* know what I'm doing and why I'm here. Whether it takes my life in the doing will not deter me from seeing my mission through. *You* should understand that sort of duty well enough." She straightened her shoulders and nodded at him. "You may go. I will take Aife to the last row, gain the powers the White Queen promised, and do what must be done to help us all."

Hook shook his head sadly. "Mortals cannot play in the games of Shepherds, or they will end up like the Jabberwocky." Wendy and I jumped at his casual mention of the dragon's name, knowing full well the potential it had for summoning him when he was so close by.

"Don't say his name," she hissed at Hook, who merely gritted his teeth and nodded. He took a step forward, and I stepped in front of Alice again.

He laughed sardonically. "Do you think to stop me from protecting my charge?" he asked. "I have searched across my country, the Wasteland, and now the Dreamworld to find her. And now that I have found her, you think you can stop me? You're a mere boy with wings and no experience."

The familiar resentment I had come to feel toward Hook boiled over into fury. "I may not be the trained warrior that you are, but I won't let you force Alice to do something she doesn't want, if it's the last thing I do."

"So be it," Hook said darkly, pulling his sword awkwardly with his left hand and surging forward.

I pushed Alice back, drawing the pixie-spelled shortsword that was part of my armor and barely meeting his blade. The weapons ground together with a sparking clash. Prickles of my sword's pixie magic prickled against the darker steel of Hook's sword, meeting its dragon-spelled magic with a teeth-grating buzz.

We pushed apart, and I realized that as good as Hook was, he was tired, injured, and using his non-dominant arm to fight. When he fought the Jabberwocky, he had held the sword with his right arm, which he was still clutching to his chest. *Perhaps it will all be enough,* I thought, running through a list of spells that would incapacitate him so I could grab Alice and run.

"Alice and Wendy," I called out as Hook and I circled each other. "On my word, I want you to grab Aife and be ready to run. We have to get to the last row."

"Why?" Wendy asked calmly, drawing a surprised glance from me—which drew Hook's quick attack. I parried the swordstroke but received a glancing blow to the head from his right elbow that I wasn't quick enough to avoid. We broke apart, my temple throbbing, although Hook couldn't hide a grimace of pain and clutched his injured hand to his chest again. *I can use that to distract him.*

"We have to finish this mission, Wendy. She's the Red Queen!"

"Exactly," Wendy called back, "we need to finish *our* mission. If we take her back to Neverland, we can treat her wounds. In her gratitude she would surely remove the breaking spell and heal the rift with the mainland!"

I shot another startled glance in her direction, catching her feverishly determined eyes, then turned back to parry the series of strokes Hook pressed on me, my heart beating in my throat with every clash, knowing if I didn't end this in the next minute or so, he would surely get a hit in. Even using his left arm he was a better swordsman than I was, and the intensity and savagery of his attacks didn't seem like he would give mercy at the final stroke.

"You fight like a pirate," I taunted him, "not what I expected from a polished royal guard."

"Spoken like a boy," he said calmly, not even out of breath. "The first rule of combat is to survive. The first rule of royal protection is to make sure your charge is safe. You're in the way of both of those objectives right now—a warrior fights to win. Only a boy would complain about losing."

"A *man* fights with honor," I threw back at him, earning a snort from Wendy.

"Hook, if I help you win, will you help me get Aife to my jumping-off point for my world?" she called out from behind me. "I promise I won't hurt Alice," she added in a tone of mixed amusement and determination. My heart stuttered at yet another betrayal from her, sudden fear for Alice taking hold.

"Yes," Hook answered her calmly. Wendy took a step toward Alice, who was hovering near Aife and watching the fight with wide eyes.

"No!" I shouted, flinging a spell at Wendy, which Hook lunged to block with his bad hand, moving with surprising speed. The spell was intended to incapacitate Wendy, not harm her, but the heady rush of my own magic being reflected back by hook's magical armor carried a tang of something acidic with it—dragon magic.

"Your arm," I gasped, moving quickly to put my body between Alice and the others. "You were bitten by the dragon!"

Wendy whipped her head around to stare at Hook in horror, momentarily stopping her advance toward my wife. "You were poisoned?" she demanded.

Hook tightened his scowl. "It doesn't matter. I have to get her home before I die."

"Where were you bitten?" Wendy demanded, taking a step toward my opponent. He kept his body toward me, but I could tell his attention was being drawn in by my one-time friend.

"My hand, but I know it will begin moving up my arm soon," he answered her, glancing back at me. His step faltered at her pained cry, and I took the opportunity to strike.

My pixie-spelled sword struck through Hook's armor like butter. After all, they were both created with my magic and the magic of my lineage, which was my poisoned birthright.

It cut cleanly, scattering sparks as it swept through his wrist. Happily for him, it didn't meet even a trace of dragon magic, proving the poison was still contained down in his hand. Hook cried out in horror, but swept at me with his left hand as only a swordsman trained with both hands could, the sword piercing the armor on my shoulder as I leaped backward, but sparing my flesh.

"Hook!" Wendy screamed as I stumbled back toward Alice and Aife. I pulled Aife, still cloaked with Hook's spell but just visible if you knew where to look, onto my shoulder, then gathered Alice awkwardly to me as well.

I sprang into the air, glancing back to see Wendy clutching a handkerchief to Hook's stump in a vain attempt to stem the bleeding. I felt Alice add a feeble cloaking spell of her own to the three of us just as a low chuckle reverberated around the clearing, and a grizzled-looking man stepped into it, one of his eyes damaged and bleeding.

"When I'm done with you, perhaps I'll go find that faerie to punish him for taking my revenge," the man said, sending a shiver down my spine. "But there's more vengeance to be had here, I think."

I flew as swiftly as I could, trusting Alice's spell to cover us as I rose above the treetops and toward the last row.

CHAPTER TWENTY-FIVE

Alice

Hook's betrayal weighed on me as Peter flew us doggedly toward the next row. I understood why he did it, having known him long enough to understand that the cornerstone of his character was an ironclad sense of honor and duty. His devotion to the queen was unwavering, and when my will conflicted with direct orders from her, I would always come second. It was as it should be.

It still hurt.

The air was cold as we rushed through it, and we kept warm through body heat alone. Peter clutched me to his chest, and the Red Queen hung ignobly over his shoulder next to me. I had wrapped one arm around his neck and kept the other over her waist to help keep her steady. The rest of my energy was spent maintaining the cloaking spell for all three of us. I had nothing left for warmth. Neither did Peter, apparently, as he was struggling to keep us aloft using his new wings.

After an agonizing length of time, the river came into sight and Peter's wings dipped alarmingly. He recovered quickly but the strain on his face made me nervous.

"Find a place to put us down," I instructed him. "We can

walk the rest of the way." He nodded, dipping unexpectedly once more before starting a controlled descent to a little clearing, not far from the edge of the trees.

He set us down with a thump, collapsing as soon as our feet hit the ground. I half propped him up, and he managed to stay upright as we lowered Aife down carefully. As soon as she was settled we both flopped down to sit on the ground next to her. Peter fluttered his wings with a groan, then gradually made them vanish, a grimace on his face.

"That's handy," I commented thoughtfully. "Then you won't bump into things when you're indoors."

Peter chuckled, resting his forehead against mine. "Your curious mind never ceases to surprise me," he said quietly. "Despite all the violence we've seen in the last few hours, you're still amazed by the simple things."

I grinned. "Well, we've only known each other for a few days, husband. I wouldn't expect you to know all the workings of my rather strange mind in such a short time."

"Strange?" he asked with raised eyebrows. "I don't know about that. Complicated, perhaps."

I smiled. "Complications are interesting in other people, but in oneself they can be tedious."

"Well, thankfully, I'm a simple man. I like fun, and lots of it. And you," he amended with a decisive nod. "And that's all there is."

I laughed, but before I could respond, a groan sounded from Aife's direction. We both turned in her direction, and I leaned over her, pressing the back of my hand to her forehead.

"Aife?" I asked anxiously. Her eyes fluttered open.

"Are we there?" she whispered. I shook my head.

"We're close. Very close. We just need to cross the last river, and then we'll be in the last row. After that—" I shook my head. "I'm hoping everything else becomes clear. Can you walk?" I added, feeling more anxious by the minute with our destination so close.

"Give me a minute, and I'm sure I can," she replied, closing her eyes once more. I cast an anxious look at Peter, who grimaced, then began pushing himself up to stand. He was obviously exhausted but found strength somewhere. I would too. We all would.

We hovered worriedly as the Red Queen took her time trying to regain some strength. I told them of everything that had happened during their absence in the last row, including the still confusing prophecy that the White King had given me. Peter didn't understand a word of it either, and Aife said she would have to think on it. Before we could catch her up on they events with the Jabberwocky, she pushed herself up and stood before us, broken, but upright.

At least for a moment. She started trembling alarmingly, so we both rushed forward, letting her sling one arm around each of our shoulders. As one, we began to walk toward the river.

Thankfully the river water here was broad but shallow, and the riverbed seemed to be more sandy than muddy. Aife gained strength as we walked, and by the time we stepped out of the water on the other side, she was able to move on her own again.

We had finally made it to the last row. We looked up to find a vast, high-roofed stone building in front of us, its enormous wooden doors closed tight. In front of the doors, on a stone plinth, was a crown of the stately, rather than pretty, variety.

"Is that—" I started, just as Peter said, "Put that on—"

I shared a grin with him as Aife said tiredly, "The crown is for you, Alice, if you choose to take up the mantle of your heritage and wear it. Even now, it's not too late to turn back. But once you place it on your head, there will be no ridding yourself of it—even when you take it off."

I swallowed heavily, the smile dropping from my face. I had gotten more than a taste of what that crown might entail, and I was starting to suspect it went beyond gaining mastery of the Dreamworld. What would happen when I put it on? Would the Jabberwocky come for me? Other horrors? What of the third sister—Adora, the Queen of Hearts? We had escaped her notice thus far, but would she feel it when I took up my crown? *I could stand here all day asking questions,* the pesky little unafraid part of my brain interjected, *but the result will remain the same. I'm going to do my part, whatever the cost.*

I walked toward the plinth, stopping to stare at the crown and shooting a wide-eyed look at Peter. He seemed to understand innately, stepping up and coming to stand behind me, his hands on my shoulders. "I'm with you, and I will be until the day we die," he said simply, neither urging me on or warning me off. He was simply there.

I drew a deep breath, then let it out—releasing all my worries and the weight of this moment. Then plucked the crown from its stand and placed it on my head.

The doors to the great hall blew open at that moment, the sound of revelry and merriment spilling out at an obscene volume, especially since the row had been deadly quiet a moment before.

"She's here!" someone shouted. "She's arrived!"

A stream of people, some half animal, like the pages in my mythology books, some perfectly human-looking save a strange color hair or overly large ears or some such. All were bedecked in finery and had clearly been sampling the hall's wine, given their flushed and grinning faces. They ushered us in, though Peter and I were careful to keep the still tired Aife between us so we all would stay together.

The flow of revelers ushered us toward a dais at the end of a great hall, and there, sitting on one of three thrones, was the White Queen, looking as dazed as I had first seen her, her hair and clothing haphazard at best, her ethereal stillness creating a void of merriment around her. She was surveying the scene with bewildered eyes that cleared upon seeing us.

As we reached the front, she sprang up, tears spilling down her cheeks as she held her hands out to her sister. Aife also had tears in her eyes, which overflowed as the White Queen's hands passed through her own, a reminder that she wasn't truly here in the Dreamworld.

"Sister," Aife said sadly. "What have you done?"

The White Queen shook her head, "I don't know. I—I can't *remember*. But surely—surely I only did what I had to?" she asked tremulously, picking nervously at her sleeves. "But, I do remember this—three queens to sit on the thrones, and hope renewed for everyone," she recited as if sitting for an exam. "It doesn't *really* rhyme. I only hope it is us three queens and not some others."

I blinked at that, a sudden desire to laugh sweeping over me. *Perhaps the White Queen, in her vagueness, told the wrong person about the quest, and it was never supposed to be me after all.*

Well, it was too late for that. Peter and I ushered the Red Queen over to the throne on the right, which was worked in red and gold and clearly meant for her. The White Queen sat back down in her unearthly white one. I hesitated momentarily, looking at the center throne, which swirled in greens, blues, whites, and gold.

"Like the colors of your wings," I whispered to Peter, who shrugged his shoulders.

"Sit," he urged me. "I'll stand behind and watch over you—just in case."

I nodded, then did as he said.

Instantly the raucous celebrations rose in volume, the noise almost painful. There was music and dancing, and although the revelers largely ignored us, they drank our health loudly and often.

"I think," the White Queen said tremulously, a hand pressed to her temple, "I think it best if we give her our power, sister. It seems as though that's what we should do, though I can't quite remember why."

Aife nodded tiredly. "Yes, sister. I'm beginning to see it now. We had planned to do so for Adora at her wedding feast, but the day never came, and all was lost before the balance could be restored. Perhaps—" she looked thoughtfully at me, "perhaps now we have a last chance. A hope indeed, before ruin is complete. Give me your hand, child," she said, and as she took hold of my fingers, I felt the White Queen's ghostly touch on my other hand, shivering a little.

A moment later, I flinched as their power entered me, and I was reminded of the Steward's language spell. But where his was a flow of words and meaning—theirs was a deluge of knowledge and magic. It was all goodness and light and everything right with the world, each Queen's magic good in it's own way—but so overwhelming as to tear apart every little piece of me, the fabric of my mind and pieces of my soul. I let it come, making room for everything they would give me and retreating further and further within myself to escape the sheer weight of it.

I felt myself becoming lost under it all and started to panic, drowning in the thought that I might not know myself anymore, now that I had the magic and knowledge—or at least some of it—of these two ancient beings.

As the panic started to consume me, I bumped into a homely little corner of my heart and recognized my connection with Peter. It glowed nicely amidst the maelstrom of magic within me, and I stepped close to it. It felt as though he had his arms around my shoulders, pressing his cheek against mine and whispering encouragement in my ear. I sank into that image, and after a time, I realized it wasn't just an image in my mind but really happening.

The magic had stopped, and although I didn't feel quite comfortable, I was myself again—with an unexplored landscape of knowledge and power within. And Peter. Always Peter.

CHAPTER TWENTY-SIX

Peter

Alice seemed to come back to herself as I soothed her, her grip on my forearms relaxing into something more affectionate than the death grip it had been for the past ten minutes or more.

The revelry roared around us, a continual swirl of joyful cries, frenzied movement, and a mix of scents from the food and drink being alternately consumed and spilled. It was absurd, considering the subjects of the revelers' joy were currently slumped on their thrones, either unconscious or nearly so.

Since Alice was starting to come around, the absurdity of the situation provoked a half smile on my face rather than a rising irritation, and I watched intently as Alice's eyes cleared, and she sat up a little straighter.

"What happened?" I asked her, but she shook her head mutely, dislodging her crown slightly so it sat at an awkward angle on her head. With a huff, she reached up and pulled the ugly thing off her head and flung it away. We both watched in surprise as it faded into nothingness almost as soon as it left her hand, then reappeared on her head.

"Okayyyy," I said as Alice took it off again in frustration, dropping it to the floor only to have it reappear on her head. "Here, try putting it in my satchel," I said quickly, as she took it off her head a third time and prepared to throw it once more. "Maybe it just needs to stay near you?" She handed it over, and I opened my bag, dropping the offending article inside and laughing as it landed next to the riding helmet she had given me to hold so long ago. "If for no other reason, it seems you should keep me around to hold offending articles of headwear," I said as the crown stayed in my bag instead of reappearing on her head.

Alice grinned at me as I closed the bag and resettled it at my waist. "A hitherto unthought of reason for having a husband," she quipped, then looked around the hall.

"The Shepherds seem weak," I said as she frowned at the White Queen, whose head practically lolled on Alice's shoulder. The Red Queen seemed a little more lucid, though her pained and haunted expression was back, casting shadows on the hollows of her face.

"Yes, they—" Alice started to respond, then cut off suddenly, clutching her head. I gripped her arms again, fear engulfing me in an instant. The crown hadn't come back—maybe she was in pain because she would have to wear it all the time as the other Queens seemed to do?

"What's wrong?" I demanded. "What can I do?" I reached out to the connection between us that was strengthening all the time, but felt nothing like the swirl of heavy power that had been pulsing through it while the Shepherds were doing whatever they had done.

Alice shook her head, then turned and looked over to one side of the dais. I followed her gaze, and my mouth dropped open. A seam was opening in the air, a few feet away from the Red Queen, who was gazing at it blearily. A figure stood on the other side, a weary looking woman with absurdly long golden hair and a man hovering just behind her.

"The weak spot," I said hoarsely, remembering the White Queen's words from what felt like a lifetime ago. "The passage between worlds."

I glanced at Alice, then hesitated at the look of intense longing and vulnerability that overtook her face.

"Persi," she whispered, and my heart broke at the mingled longing, relief, and wistful hope her voice held. I knew she cherished her sister—cherished her so much that she jumped through a dark mirror into a world she knew nothing about to find her. And I remembered, too, the agony of her choice to abandon that search in favor of completing the White Queen's mission. Now, at last, we were at the final moment of both missions. She had one chance now, as the seam was almost wide enough for a person to squeeze through, the rippling wrongness making it hard to look at.

"Let me help," I urged her, letting go of Alice's arms and rushing to help get Aife upright. The longing on Alice's face made it clear that she was thinking of jumping through the tear and reuniting with her long-lost sister. But I also knew the passage would last only a moment, and she would always regret stumbling at the last moment in her mission.

A raven swooped from the rafters above us, cawing loudly and hurtling toward the rip in the Dreamworld. Its noisy flight seemed to snap Alice out of her feelings, and as she watched the raven's flight through the tear, she locked eyes with her sister.

"Save her!" she yelled to Persi, shoving Aife through the seam, then letting out a pained sob as it sealed instantly behind the Red Queen, disappearing as if it had never been.

Alice went very white, almost as white as the remaining Shepherd next to her. I stepped closer, putting my hand on her shoulder and pressing a quick kiss to the top of her head.

"Well, that's done," I said lightly, hoping to lighten the mood slightly, impossible task though it would be. "The thing with the raven was unexpected. Honestly, it looked like a smaller version of the one that chased us into Aife's weird house—jail—torture-meadow—place."

Alice blinked at me, then let out a peal of laughter that verged on the hysterical. "I guess," she gasped out, wiping away tears, "I guess there isn't a better description of that place than torture-meadow." She shivered, sobering again. "How horrible it was."

"Yes. This whole place has become horrible to me, though it used to be my escape." A sudden longing for Neverland overtook me—Neverland and its loud innocence, the carefree lives that most led. In a flash, I understood the sacrifice my ancestors made and which my mother insisted on. The life and sanity of one person for the safety of all the others, little though some wanted it. We knew no such horrors as there were in the Dreamland, though there was darkness at home of another kind. *It would be a perfect place for Alice to recuperate, and if I could bring the White Queen, she could see her daughter.*

"Alice, I think we should go to Neverland," I told her excitedly. "You can rest there, and if we bring the White Queen with us, we could reunite her with her daughter, who has been hidden away there since the breaking—"

"What?" Alice asked, blinking and sitting a little straighter on her throne. "Go to your home? Wait—did you say the White Queen's daughter is there?"

"Yes," I admitted sheepishly, "she's the one my mother has been trying to make me—"

Alice groaned. "Don't say it. I have to compete with the only daughter of the White King and Queen?"

"No!" I protested. "There's no competition. You already have my heart in a way no one else ever has. She's a friend—" I stopped, considering. "Well, not really a friend. She's annoying, actually, but she's not *not* a friend, if that makes sense...."

Alice snorted. "With you, yes, that makes sense. Well, if you can get us there, I would like to go. As long as my mission here is truly over," she added anxiously, turning to the White Queen, whose eyes had fluttered open as we talked. "Is my part here done?"

The queen crooked a sad half-smile at her. "Done? None of our parts are ever done until we are called home to the Starlight Havens by the Creator." She patted Alice's hand wearily. "You must walk through the door in front of you, child, and do what you think is right." Alice nodded, then stood up, motioning me forward.

"Tell her your plan then, Peter," she urged, and I knelt by the queen's side.

"Your Majesty, I have news that may shock you," I said sheepishly. "I should have said something earlier, but, well, I didn't. It's about your daughter—"

"I forgot!" Alice interjected, pressing her hands against her cheeks. "I saw the White King too, and your steward! I promised him I would mention him to you if I saw you again. Steward Humphrey. And the White King hasn't forgotten you, your majesty—"

"Who?" the White Queen asked confusedly, her papery brow wrinkling. Alice gaped at her in astonishment.

"Your...your family," I replied, echoing her confusion. "I know where your daughter is. She's safe and I can bring you to her—if we can find a way to keep you with us while we fly."

"Ah yes, flying. It's quite good for the spirit, isn't it? But I can't go with you, boy. I—well, I can't remember why, but I know I'm bound here. Or at least, this part of me is. I seem to remember that—oh well, it's all slipping from my mind now. I can't remember anything really." She shook her head. "I think I'll be going now." With that, she faded from sight, thinning and dispersing in front of my eyes with shocking speed.

*I hadn't even told her **where** her daughter was*, I realized. *Although she'd probably forget it soon enough anyway.* Her condition was curious, and I wondered if she was even fully a Shepherd anymore.

I turned back to Alice, only to find she wasn't right behind me as I thought. A glance around revealed she was only a few yards away, stepping through a door with her name emblazoned in glowing gold over the lintel that had appeared exactly where the seam between worlds had been not long ago.

"Alice!" I shouted, lunging toward her, but the door slammed shut, locking me out.

CHAPTER TWENTY-SEVEN

Alice

I opened my eyes slowly, taking in the soft morning light casting a happy glow around my old tower bedroom. The scent of roses hung around the air, slightly cloying but not enough to disrupt the usual smells of books and clean linen I remembered so well. It's so nice to be home, I thought sleepily, stretching my arms and smiling at the familiar surroundings.

I've been away for much too long. To think I had wanted to escape—I frowned, trying to remember what I had wanted to escape from, but not quite able to think of it. It had been something unpleasant, but not terrible. I had asked for permission to go—where?

To Deerbold, I remembered suddenly. But now, such a trip felt silly. Traveling all that way into the northern wilds. I shook my head.

"All that bother and fuss just because I wasn't feeling myself. Silly Alice." I sat up and swung my legs out of my bed, grabbing the lace-lined white robe that hung from my bedpost and wrapping it around me. "I'll go catch Grandmother in the breakfast room before court starts today and tell her I changed my mind." But as I took a few steps toward my bedroom door, my feet faltered, and I slowly turned back to face my room, trying to remember what I was doing.

I stood frowning for a moment, then shrugged, smiling at the way the soft morning light cast a happy glow around my old tower room. *It's so nice to be home.* I sighed happily, tripping over to the painted vanity on the other side of my room. I sat down with a flounce, pulling out the hair ribbons holding my braid in place, and dropping them into one of the little drawers before pulling my horsehair brush out of another one and running it through my long blonde hair.

I looked at my reflection, and my hand slowed as I pulled the hairbrush through the ends of my hair. "You're back," I said to the Lady in the Mirror, frowning at the impolite revulsion I felt at her appearance and trying not to let it show on my face.

The woman must have seen some of it because she tutted at me, her dark eyebrows raising and her full dark lips twisting into a mocking smile. "You have been dreaming again, haven't you, Alice?" she asked with a kindly censure that sounded nice but felt oily. "One imagines you would have left that sort of thing behind when you grew up. But you haven't, have you?"

I set the brush down on my vanity, though I kept a grip on it as I frowned at the woman, so beautiful and different from myself. "Surely everyone dreams," I said finally, and the dark-haired lady—who seemed *so* familiar—tilted her head back in a tinkling laugh.

"To be sure, my dear, but not the way *you* do. For most of us, it's about everyday things, like the work we have to do or the ball we attended last night. But that's not what you dreamed of, was it, darling?" she asked coaxingly.

I shook my head slowly, oddly resistant to prolonging my conversation with this person, though she seemed to be very familiar with me and my ways. *Perhaps I should go get*—I paused. Who would I go get? There was no one else—there was nothing else but here. Only me, in this tower room—me and this woman who looked fair but felt foul.

"Well, you had better tell me all about it, Alice," she urged firmly. "You know that's the best way. Tell every detail, and as the words leave you, so will the dreams, and then you can get on with your day."

I nodded slowly, seeing the logic of her advice but still reluctant to part with my dreams. They had been horrible in some ways, but they had been my own. I scrunched my nose up, trying to think back. "There was a creature—a horrible dragon called a...a, oh, what was it?" I said slowly, then snapping my fingers. "A Jabberwocky. And it tried to kill me, and I really thought it *would*, but then *he* came—" I broke off, suddenly and violently loath to share *him* with this beautiful woman, even if he was just a dream.

"Who?" the woman prompted, leaning eagerly toward the mirror. "This is all so interesting, little Alice, do tell," she ordered. An odd compulsion opened my mouth, but I shut it again, looking at her with a little worm of curiosity making its way through my brain.

"Well," I said slowly, unable to keep from speaking entirely, but just strong enough to steer my words away from *him*, who I wanted to keep to myself. "It was all about queens, really, and a chessboard. There were *several* queens, and it's all a bit hard to keep track of."

A trilling laugh echoed through the mirror. "Your dreams always are, Alice. All the better to tell them to me, my dear, so I can help keep it straight. Now, this is very important: *which* queens did you meet? There are so many these days; I should like to have a little picture in mind about whom you are speaking of."

I took a moment to picture the queens, the images of them sitting upon their thrones on either side of me coalescing slowly but surely in my memory. The dream, slow to grow started to become more and more vivid—more like a true memory, not a dream-one.

"It was you, wasn't it?" I asked thoughtfully, the images filtering through my mind. "*You* were the one they spoke of. You sort of look like them—the two sister queens. And they said we could heal what was once broken, so when we sat on the thrones, they shared with me their power—"

"They did what?" the woman screeched, her perfect features twisting into a rage so pure, I could feel it even through the mirror. I pushed my stool back, almost stumbling as I scrambled up and backed away from the mirror.

My head was suddenly clear, and I *knew* I wasn't really in my room at the castle. I had been at Deerbold, and then Cara's, and then...then the Dreamworld, where everything had changed. I was no longer the Alice I once was; this place was no longer in my future. My frilly nightgown and robe were merely tricks of whatever spell had been cast on me. As I thought it, my dirty riding clothes reappeared on my body, boots and all.

"Sit back down," the woman in the mirror commanded harshly, her voice reaching out to me with silken bonds to ensnare my will again. I recognized her now, the knowledge and magic her sisters had given me solidifying in my mind.

"No, Adora, I won't," I said briskly. "That's who you are, aren't you? One of the Ancient Shepherds, the Queen of Hearts." I laughed sadly as a startled look crossed her face. "You were supposed to be the best of them, the one who brought the whole world together in love. That's what the Book of Hearts says—the heart leads with love and strengthens the bonds between us. But you didn't, did you? You're the one who broke everything in the end."

The queen snarled, then pushed forward, a bolt of fear striking through my heart as I realized she was somehow moving *through* the mirror. *It's just like Cara's mirror*, I realized belatedly.

"And you seek to supplant me," she laughed darkly, stepping fully into my fake room, her presence darkening it and casting the gloom of a cage over it. "Let us test our powers then, little usurper, and we will see who is the true Queen of Hearts."

I stepped backward, my back hitting the door I had entered through.

"That's right, child," the queen spat. "There's nowhere to run. It's time I ended you."

I felt her gather her power, and pressed myself against the door as my mind raced through every protective spell I had learned since I was a child, which Hook had made me practice weekly when he took over as my guard, even though it wasn't strictly necessary. None of them would be powerful enough to withstand a Shepherd, I knew. *All that practice and for nothing*, I thought desperately as memories of his strict lessons ran through my mind.

First, run if you are able, Hook's deep voice filtered through my memory. *If you can escape without magic, do it. Then you'll be safe and won't have used up any power. Only fight if you must.*

My hand scrabbled behind me, hitting the metal doorknob with a smack. I grasped it tightly, my sweaty palm slipping, so I turned to twist it with both hands, my eyes still trained on the dark queen.

Her mouth opened as the door gave. I tumbled through it, back into the noisy banquet hall, and straight into Peter's arms. With a great heave, I pushed the door shut with my shoulder, Peter helping as the Queen of Hearts released her spell. I felt it hit the closed door, which shuddered, then disappeared, my name in gold lettering vanishing last with a friendly wink.

I collapsed in a shaking heap, sick of the twists and turns of the Dreamworld and the games of the queens. "Let's go home," I told Peter. "Take me to Neverland. Please."

CHAPTER TWENTY-EIGHT

Peter

"I couldn't have dreamed of a more beautiful place," Alice breathed as I set us down on a white sand beach, the turquoise water breaking in gentle foamy waves a few feet away. She breathed in deeply, relaxing for what felt like the first time since I'd left her on shore in the Steward's row.

"It is now that you're here," I said playfully, drawing a laugh, but I meant it. All around us, the air felt like a gentle, warm embrace, and the beach stretched between the crystalline water and a vivid wall of green dotted with huge flowers in brilliant hues. Everything was beautiful, and Alice was the most beautiful of all—inside and out.

She leaned back into my embrace, drinking in the peace and harmony that lay like a blanket over the island. "We're home," I murmured, and she hummed her agreement.

This is what the Dreamworld should be like, I thought idly, then voiced my thoughts to Alice. "I was just thinking that *this* is what the Dreamworld should be like—a haven of beauty and rest, not the nightmare we just left."

She sighed. "I agree. And I think that's what the Dreamworld *wants* to be, or at least parts of it still want to be like that. But other parts have been trampled by the nightmares of powerful beings for so long that it can't heal itself or shape what happens with its own nature. It needs a guiding hand."

"Maybe you could be that guiding hand," I prompted. "Use your newly acquired powers. After a rest here, of course."

"I don't think I could do it on my own," she mused.

"I would help, of course, in any way I can," I assured her quickly. "I told you I'd never leave your side."

She squeezed my arm. "I trust you. But that's not what I meant. I...I'm still sifting through everything the Red and White Queens gave me, but I have memories—or someone's memories—that the Dreamworld was supposed to be ruled over and Shepherded by the White Queen's daughter. Creator knows where she is or what she's like now, but I can't help feeling that if we found her, she would be better suited to healing that place." She turned to me suddenly. "Didn't you say she was here?" she demanded. "Do you know where she might be? I have that message to give her, from her father."

"Yes, I know where's she is, but she's never mentioned that she was supposed to be Queen of the Dreamworld," I said doubtfully. "But I guess she's a sort of Shepherd since her parents both were. I guess I never thought of it that way." Another thing occurred to me. "The audacity of my mother! Trying to force a wedding between a Shepherd and me!" I shook my head. "Introducing my new wife to my mother is going to be interesting, no matter what mood she's in."

"As much as I'm looking forward to meeting my future mother-in-law, that's merely a side quest," she said with raised eyebrows. "I promised back at the queen's rock I would help you break the hold Neverland has on you. I meant it," she said fiercely.

I nodded solemnly. "I know you did. And if anyone can do it, we can. But I still don't have even the slightest idea of how it can be done. In the meantime, I can take you to meet Lily, and we can bring news of the Shepherds and your newly acquired, or awakened, or whatever, magic."

"Can we fly?" Alice asked, smiling up at me. I grinned, glad I didn't even need pixie magic to grant her request.

"Any excuse to hold you close, wife," I answered, gathering her in my arms and kissing her with the promise of a lifetime of love and adventure. "Hold on tight!" And she did.

EPILOGUE

"Right," I said decisively, realizing I would have to take charge based on the growing pallor on Hook's face. From the blood loss, not fear, I noted admiringly. He was in a bad way, and I also felt a little guilty for distracting him in his fight with Peter, causing the loss of his hand.

Peter! I growled in my head. He was always an idiot. There was a time I'd hoped he would be *my* idiot. After I realized that wasn't likely to happen, I still tried to keep him by my side, hoping that a friend in the Faerie court would help—especially once he became The Pixie. But now he was married, and my attempt to betray his wife was just the sort of thing he'd hold a grudge over.

I finished tying off the makeshift tourniquet on Hook's wrist while the strange man prattled on a few yards away. He was fairly dripping with power, though he looked like he could use a few good meals and a nap that lasted for a year. *Men never seem to take care of themselves without a good woman around. They've only survived this far because they have a strange knack for conquering our hearts, and once ensnared, we never get them back. Well, **I** won't be trapped that way.*

I gave Hook a quick once over as I patted my jacket pockets. He looked like he'd survive if I could get him back to Neverland and use one of those blasted healing potions. It wouldn't restore his hand, unfortunately, but better having no hand than dragon poison and a sure death. When I had checked earlier, it seemed like Peter had struck far enough up the wrist that he had cut off all the poison. *The only good thing he ever did for someone else*, I thought sourly. The man at the edge of the clearing took a step forward, and some of his whining finally filtered through my mind as Hook brought his sword up in preparation for an attack.

"Well, you probably talked your poor wife half insane to begin with, judging by all the nonsense you've been spewing since you got here. Having done a poor job at that—and ruined her body with a ship's worth full of kids, if I had to guess—you've run off to enjoy yourself in the Dreamworld. When you couldn't get back, you decided to blame her and inflict all the misery you used to give her on anyone else who crossed your path," I scolded him as I patted the pockets in my trousers, finally finding the shape I wanted and blessed myself for slipping it into my trousers earlier just in case. "What's that?" I asked, as a distraction as I pulled my grenade out, tipping my chin to a medallion necklace with an old-fashioned compass rose emblazoned on it.

The Red King stopped a foot or two away and looked down in a daze. "My necklace," he said enigmatically, his tone strikingly different from the mocking darkness it held before. "My idea, to heal the rift the elves created—to bring them home across the waves, by starlight and magic. My brothers-in-law helped me make it back before—"

"Sounds like *just* what I was looking for," I said breezily, smiling at the astonished looks I got from both the Jabberwocky and Hook. "So I'll be having it," I said, snatching the medallion from his neck—which gave way with surprising ease though it hung from a golden chain. "In return, you can have this."

I managed to avoid fumbling the medallion as I turned the top of the grenade, releasing the starter liquid into the main chamber, then tossed it to the one-eyed Red King—looping my arm around Hook's waist in the same moment and releasing the last bit of pixie dust I had been holding in my free hand over both of us. *I hope it's enough*, I thought as I sprung us both into the air. Before the Red King could change forms and follow, my grenade went off, injuring him—though probably not killing him as it would a normal man—and spewing clouds of noxious smoke to obscure our flight.

I ignored Hook's questions as I pressed upward through the gloom of the Dreamworld, concentrating on thoughts of Neverland and Pirate Cove, only breathing a sigh of relief when the stars appeared. I took a moment to reorient myself, found the right ones, and laughed as we flew, finally relaxing in the knowledge that the Red King—or any other Dreamworld creature—couldn't follow us. Not without pixie dust.

"Where are you taking us?" Hook asked again, and I finally noticed he had slumped against me, probably trying to hide that he was close to passing out. I glanced at the place where his hand should be and grimaced. The handkerchief was stained completely red, although no drops of blood escaped it.

"I won't let you fall if you pass out," I reassured him, earning a laughing snort. I stared up into his brown eyes, curling one side of my mouth into an answering smile. "Although," I continued roguishly, "I'd miss seeing your eyes fall out of your head on your first glimpse of the island."

The small smile on his face disappeared into a thoughtful frown. "We're going to your island?"

I laughed again. "If it were my island, things would be vastly different than they are now. But yes, we're going to the island where I live. Now hush for a minute," I demanded, returning my focus to our flight and the limited control I had over the rapidly depleting pixie dust.

The star I knew to be Neverland grew rapidly at the rate we were traveling. I kept us angled properly, making adjustments to my usual speed since I was carrying another person. Hook craned his neck around awkwardly to try and catch a glimpse of what I was focused on until I tutted at him. He snapped back around with a surprised look on his face, then relaxed fully after a moment, gingerly letting his chin rest on the top of my head and tightening his arms around me in a warm embrace that I liked too much. *He's just another casualty of fights you didn't want that needs taken care of,* I reminded myself. *Nothing more.*

"Now you can look," I told him as the island shifted entirely into view, and our descent began to slow. He turned his neck again, this time resting his cheek along my temple in a gesture that was probably more comfortable than last time, but felt more intimate than I would have thought.

"It's—it's startling," he said at last, and I hummed in agreement.

"Very startling the first time you see it, although few have left. Me and Peter, curse him, may be the only two since it was first sundered. When you're down there, you don't know the whole place is floating in a sea of stars."

Hook didn't respond, merely watched our descent, resting his cheek along my temple as if it belonged there. Since he was injured, I allowed the gesture of closeness when I normally would have put him right into his place. Once we landed, I would hand him over to a sawbones, make sure he was settled with some occupation, and then contact my parents if I could. After that, he'd be on his own. With a face like his, he'd be snapped up by some girl before long.

The thought made me oddly wistful, which was annoying and unhelpful, so I pushed it aside and braced for landing as I felt the last of the pixie dust give out. We weren't quite on the ground yet, so we fell the last foot or two, landing in a tumbled heap on the jungle grass atop the bluff surrounding Pirate's Cove.

I somehow ended up on top of him, with Hook flat on his back, staring at me with a dazed expression. *Poor guy has been so battered and bruised the last few hours that he's going to need every potion we have in port,* I thought as I gave him a quick once over. Nothing seemed worse than it had been before, so I grinned down at his wide eyes.

"Welcome to Neverland, Captain Hook. I think we'll find some use for you in Pirate's Cove."

NEXT BOOK IN THIS SERIES

Coming Soon! Read Wendy and Captain Hook's story as they restore Neverland to it's rightful place, and change the future of Istoire forever.

BOOKS BY THIS AUTHOR

Belle & Beast

A war hero. A prince with a secret. A distressed damsel intent on beating the odds. They're not the fairytale characters you're used to.

After proving himself a hero during the war, Eddie Marchand returns home to marry his childhood sweetheart, Lady Belle. Lady Belle chafes at the life she's led in a quiet backwater, patiently waiting to restore her family's fortune. When a beastly Prince disrupts their lives attempting to protect his secret, Belle makes a choice that plunges her into a world of magic and mystery. Will Eddie save his childhood sweetheart from a life of horror? Will the Prince resist the fate foretold to him? Can Belle crack the secrets of her new home and save them all? The threat of war is building again. This time, the entire continent may be at stake unless long buried secrets are uncovered.

Belle & Beast is a clean, fantasy-romance retelling of the French fairytale, Beauty & the Beast. It is the first book in the Istoire Awakens series, but can be enjoyed as a standalone.

The Red Rider

The day Red walked through the woods to meet her grandmother was the day her childhood ended. But she's not a little girl anymore.

RED: I not only survived the revolution—I thrived. I'm now sister to the Duke and Duchess of Sherwood, Captain of an elite border unit, and revered by the people as The Red Rider—the one who turned the tide from the dark days of civil war. But even though I've conquered the monsters of my past, shadows have started creeping into my present. When I'm tasked with guarding a tight-laced Pelerine soldier, his contempt for me and my country makes me see red. But as we start to become friends, I find myself relying on him more and more.

EDDIE: I woke up to a brutal reality after the Battle of Asielboix. Alone and wounded in potentially hostile territory, I'm at the mercy of the intriguing and dangerous Captain Hood. She's everything I should hate, but I can't deny that I'm drawn to her. We're bound together for now, and sparks are flying as we force each other to confront our demons. It's hard for me to admit—but I'm hoping one of those sparks ignites something powerful. When Red is called upon to right the wrong of her only failure, Eddie turns out to be the one person who can stand by her side through it—if they can trust each other first.

The Red Rider is a clean fantasy-romance retelling of the French fairytale, Little Red Riding Hood. It is the second book in the Istoire Awakens series, and although it can be read as a standalone, it is better enjoyed as part of the series.

Glass Slipper

Growing up in the midst of tragedy and triumph, Ella knows better than anyone that what's inside a person counts more than their appearance. Even so, a pretty dress and a pair of oddly beautiful glass slippers change her life more than she ever imagined.

ELLA: Ever since my father died, I've been so busy running my ancestral estate and caring for family that I haven't had time for romance. But a chance meeting has me re-thinking whether I have room in my future for love. Every time I'm with Luca I'm convinced we can take on any challenge life throws our way. And it's getting hard to ignore the way he makes my heart beat faster...

LUCA: I've always believed in love at first sight. What else would explain why the strange girl I met one time over a decade ago has never left my head (or heart)? I've finally found her again, and I'm convinced she's the one I need by my side. The only problem? She doesn't know I'm the crown prince, and she's not exactly who my parents have in mind as our next queen.

A pair of glass dancing slippers seal Ella's fate with her true love, but the very magic that binds them together drives a wedge between them; and reveals a talent Ella never wanted.

When events in Charmagne reach a tipping point, will Ella and her Prince find a way to be together? Or will their splintered relationship fracture the kingdom and continent beyond repair?

Glass Slipper is a clean fantasy-romance retelling of the classic fairytale, Cinderella. It is the third book in the Istoire Awakens series, and although it can be read as a standalone, is better enjoyed whenread as part of the series.

Snow White

In a warlike country where magic is outlawed and mages are put to death, the Snow White princess has little power to aid the suffering. An evil embedded deep within the court has grown strong enough to resist even the most powerful players of the shifting Snowdonian court. But there may be one thing it's overlooked – kindness can be a weapon too.

NIEVE: Even though I'm a princess, I've lived a quiet life. My biggest royal role is singing the Snow White song at court for Winter Solstice. All I want is to support my loved ones, and feel their love in return. That dream was shattered the day I discovered I have forbidden magic, and the depths my stepmother would reach to get rid of it. My unlikely savior is the best friend I rejected years ago. Somehow, after all this time, he's willing to risk his life to get me to safety. Does the future I thought was gone still has a chance at coming true?

ALARIC: I've been living a dangerous double life as a Snowdonian warrior-huntsmen for the last ten years, but I've abandoned it all in order to get Princess Nieve to safety. But it turns out that the refuge I brought her to may be just as dangerous as her murderous stepmother. I'll sacrifice almost anything to keep her safe, but I don't know if I'm ready to make the most dangerous sacrifice of all – my heart.

When the illusion of safety for Nieve and Alaric is suddenly shattered, will it destroy the second chance of love between them? And will Nieve find the courage to stand up for her oppressed people—even if her only weapon is the strength of her heart?

Snow White is a clean fantasy-romance retelling of the classic fairytale, Little Snow White. It is the fourth book in the Istoire Awakens series, and although it can be read as a standalone, is better enjoyed when read as part of the series.

Briar Rose

Deerbold Academy was founded to bring the ruling families of Istoire together. After years of hard work, its purpose is finally being achieved—but with a threat gathering in the Wasteland to the north, it may be too late.

Briar Rose: The Headmistresses of Deerbold Academy took me in when I was a baby: giving me a family, a home, and opportunities I never would have had otherwise. As graduation approaches I seem to be losing control. My migraines are getting stronger, my magic is getting weaker, and the future I thought I was building at the Academy feels like it's slipping away. I'm supposed to be an adult now, but instead of knowing what to do, I think I'm losing my mind. The only constant is my best friend, Prince Raleigh. He says he's in love with me, but I'm not exactly princess material and I never envisioned leaving my home in the ancient forest.

Raleigh: As sixth in line to the throne of Spindle the weight of ruling won't ever fall on my shoulders, but it doesn't mean I don't have royal duties. One of those duties sent me to Deerbold Academy to ensure it's success. I've spent the last four years and more happily fulfilling that task. As graduation approaches, I've started to realize my devotion over the years wasn't dedication to the mission, it was dedication to someone—my best friend, Briar Rose. What I feel for her isn't just friendship, it's steadfast, wholehearted love. But there are mysteries swirling at the Academy, and the more I dig, the more it seems like Briar Rose is at the center of them.

On the night of her twenty-first birthday, Briar Rose's questions are answered, and her world shattered. She's left with a clear plan that could save the continent, but the only person who believes her is Raleigh. Can they find a way to fulfill Briar Rose's vision despite the prophecy foretold at her birth? And will the feelings growing between them make them stronger, or ruin their friendship forever?

Briar Rose is a clean fantasy-romance retelling of the classic fairytale, Sleeping Beauty. It is the fifth book in the Istoire Awakens series, and although it can be read as a standalone, is better enjoyed when read as part of the series.

Rapunzel

Princess Persinette, code name Rapunzel, has been trapped in a tower deep in the Wasteland for two years. Her last companion left in a desperate bid for help. Injured and alone, she's finally succumbing to the madness of her surroundings.

Persinette: As fifth in line to the throne of Spindle, I don't have the weight of the crown on my shoulders, but I do have a responsibility to my family, and my country, that always comes first. I've dedicated my life so far to studying the biggest threat to both—the arcane and twisted magic of the Wasteland. After my last mission ended in disaster, I'm stuck in a tower with no hope of rescue. The magic here is pulling me under, and as I inevitably give in, I can't help sinking into memories of a simpler time, when my heart briefly ruled my head. But when the object of my dreams shows up for a rescue, we discover that my wounded pride isn't the only thing that was keeping us apart.

Petro: The day that Persinette rejected me and our bond was the day my heart died. As the infamous Gypsy Prince, I've traveled the continent my whole life, running from a fate that I know will eventually catch up. In the last year however, I've been focused on one thing—finding Persinette by any means necessary. When a young seer from Spindle sets me on the path to my true love, I leap at the chance. Finding her turns out to be the easy part. Getting both of us back home alive is proving almost impossible —but rekindling the fire that once burned between us may end up killing me.

As Petro and Persinette seek a way home, they discover that Persinette wasn't trapped in the Wasteland by chance, and the person who wants her body and soul isn't going to give up easily.

Rapunzel is a clean fantasy-romance retelling of the classic fairytale by the same name. It is the fifth book in the Istoire Awakens series, and although it can be read as a standalone, in order to have a full understanding of the larger story of the series it is best enjoyed when read in order.

CONNECT WITH ME

For a free novelette, and a peek into the Istoire Awakens world, sign up for my newsletter at:

https://www.rebeccafittery.com/newsletter-and-free-short-story

Website: https://www.rebeccafittery.com/

IG:https://www.instagram.com/rebecca_fittery_author/

Facebook:https://www.facebook.com/RebeccaFitteryAuthor

ACKNOWLEDGEMENTS

Thank you so much to Katherine Nadene, as always, for putting up with my insanity. And to the Foehn Wind Writers, who cheer me on both in my writing and my regular life.

Thank you also to my family. This book wandered through my brain through holidays, birthdays, school days, schedule changes, and all the other things that give a family it's structure. Thank you for ignoring the times I made a mad dash for my notebook, or stood half catatonic as I recorded an idea on my phone notes. And thank you so much for supporting me every step of the way.

Thank you last, but never least, to you dear reader. I hope you enjoyed your wanderings through another world, and getting to know these two weird and ornery characters. I'll see you in the next adventure!

ABOUT THE AUTHOR

Rebecca Fittery

Rebecca writes clean, new adult fairytale romance in a world of magic and mystery. Everyone who deserves a happy ending gets one, and even those who don't deserve one have a chance. Whether they take it or not is up to them!

She currently lives in the wilds of rural Pennsylvania with her husband, their pint sized princess and prince, and an orange tiger cat. When she's not writing, her days are spent exploring with her kids in the woods behind their house. So far they've found a fairy circle, a witch's cottage, and several perfect climbing trees.

Made in the USA
Coppell, TX
25 March 2024

30504570R00125